Silent Stranger

SILENT STRANGER

Amanda Benton

 AVON BOOKS NEW YORK

AVON BOOKS
A division of
The Hearst Corporation
1350 Avenue of the Americas
New York, New York 10019

Copyright © 1997 by Amanda Benton
Interior design by Kellan Peck
Visit our website at http://AvonBooks.com
ISBN: 0-380-97486-X

Library of Congress Cataloging in Publication Data:

Benton, Amanda.
   Silent stranger / Amanda Benton—1st ed.
      p.   cm.
Summary: Although they do not know anything about him, the mute young
man who shows up on their New York farm at Christmastime in 1813
becomes increasingly important to fourteen-year-old Jessie and her family.
[1. Frontier and pioneer life—New York (State)—Fiction. 2. United
States—History—War of 1812—Fiction. 3. New York (State)—Fiction.]
I. Title
PZ7.M5885Si   1997   97-439
                                                                        CIP

First Avon Books Printing: October 1997

AVON TRADEMARK REG. U.S. PAT. OFF. AND IN OTHER COUNTRIES, MARCA REGIS-
TRADA, HECHO EN U.S.A.

Printed in the U.S.A.

FIRST EDITION

QPM   10   9   8   7   6   5   4   3   2   1

In memory of Janet

Chapter 1

JESSICA KNEW IT was wrong not to love her grand-mother, but there was no getting around it—she did not love Grandmother Brock. She never said it aloud, but her father surely knew how she felt. Deep down, Jessica reasoned, her father had to feel the same way. He knew that Grandmother Brock blamed him for marrying Jessica's mother and taking her away from Albany. Why, Grandmother Brock treated Alva no better than a stablehand most of the time. Jessica remembered how curt and uncivil she had been to him just before they left for western New York.

The red hair in the family should have been hers instead of her older brother's, she thought. Sixteen-year-old Linus was easygoing most of the time, while Jessica, who had mousy brown hair, was always having to curb her temper and bite her tongue. Still, where Grandmother Brock was concerned, she reasoned that if her father could be patient and polite with her in the face of her rudeness, she could be, too.

She helped him compose the letter to the old lady. Alva was perfectly able to write for himself, but he said, "Your hand's finer than mine. I want it to look neat."

They stayed up late writing it by candlelight, just the two of them. Linus was up in the loft, sleeping like a stone as usual. Her mother, Ruth, was sleeping fitfully in the bedroom that adjoined the main room of the log house, still not entirely recovered from the latest bout of fever that had scared them so. Jessica couldn't remember how many months had gone by since the fevers had started. But what the illness had done to her mother was plain enough. She was so thin that her clothes hung in folds around her. Her usually thick, glossy hair was dull and lifeless, her skin pale, her cheeks sunken.

"We'll start it 'My dear mother-in-law,' " Alva said, yanking at his beard and striding up and down. Jessica brought her attention back to the task at hand and wrote the words carefully with her crow-quill pen and pokeberry ink. "I hope this letter finds you in good health and enjoying God's many blessings. We have been faring well and the farm has prospered during the time we've been here." He paused while Jessica wrote, then went on. "God has helped us make a good life for ourselves here in the western New York country. However, in recent months my dear wife's health has given us all—" He hesitated, and Jessica suggested, "Some cause for anxiety?"

"Yes. Well put. Exactly right." Jessica scratched

away while her father went on pacing, his hair pulling loose from its eelskin thong and starting to straggle. "It is on that account that I write—to suggest that you might be willing to come and carry her back to Albany, where she can spend the winter months recruiting her strength. Perhaps one of the doctors in Albany might help put her to rights, and I know she would welcome the rest. I dislike putting her in a public coach, as I wish for her to have every comfort on the journey."

Jessica's teeth clamped together. She knew what it must be costing him to write such a letter, just as she knew the satisfaction her grandmother would feel when she read it. The words "I told them so" would be on the tip of her tongue.

The next day he walked five miles to the village and left the letter at Stillwater's store with urgent instructions that it be carried by the next traveler or coach headed east. Only then did Jessica begin to think about what lay ahead—a long, cold season of loneliness with her mother far away. Giving up her lessons at Mrs. Baldwin's school—she couldn't be spared at home with her mother gone. And Christmas! How could they ever get through Christmas without her?

Grandmother Brock arrived late in October, pulling up to the log house she had never been willing to visit before in a neat carriage painted black, with thin lines of gold trim and polished leather braces. She was driven by her old servant, Jeremiah, and accompanied by a lady's maid she called Sampson, a thin, stringy woman who jumped to do her bidding. Mrs.

Brock, a small, pink-cheeked woman in stylish dark green silk, took charge at once, issuing orders and organizing the household like a general deploying troops. Women were to sleep in the house, men could manage in the barn. Sampson would help with the cooking. Mrs. Brock was obviously delighted to be taking her daughter home to Albany with her, and at once suggested that Jessica might like to come, too.

"Wouldn't you like that, my dear?" she asked. "Spend a winter in Albany? See something of society?"

Jessica was not sure what society was. She picked up Floss, hugging the cat to her tightly, and said politely, "It's kind of you to ask, Grandmother. But I don't think I can be spared here." She decided not to add any details about what that meant—tending the kitchen garden, separating the milk, churning the butter, feeding the chickens, spinning the wool, cooking the meals.

"Spared from what, for heaven's sake?" Mrs. Brock snapped. "Breaking your back with work and ruining your health just as my dear Ruth has?" But she was astute enough not to push the point at that moment. Jessica could almost see her saving some ammunition for later. Her grandmother would have liked them all to go back east, and permanently. Her own husband was a prosperous Albany merchant. Her daughter Ruth could have had any one of several town suitors who would have pleased her mother better than Alva, a handsome young man with his heart set on farming in the western reaches of New York State.

Jessica, Linus, and Ruth had lived with Grandmother Brock for a year before they all moved out west. Alva had gone ahead to buy land and build a cabin, and in all the time he was gone, Jessica never heard her grandmother say one nice thing about him. She remembered Grandmother's high, querulous voice saying to Ruth, "If you don't want to think of yourself, at least give a little thought to Jessica's future. Why, she'll be lucky to have a pair of decent shoes on her feet. And what kind of husband will she ever find out there in that godforsaken country?"

"As good as mine, I hope," Ruth had replied stoutly.

"Yes, well, that's a matter of opinion."

"I will not hear you speak disparagingly of Alva, Mother." There had been a catch in her mother's voice, as if she was trying not to cry. And Jessica was furious with her grandmother for making Ruth sad. The older woman had backed off, not pressing too hard, Jessica thought, for fear of losing the advantage she held.

When Alva came back to Albany to move them out west, Grandmother had been chilly and barely polite. He was the enemy—the man who had won her daughter and now was going to carry her off.

Little had changed in the years they'd been on the farm. Grandmother Brock began to nag at Alva shortly after she arrived. "I should think you'd find the war news most alarming," she said, her small mouth pursing. "It seems to me you must be very close to the fighting."

"No, Mother Brock. The forts are all to the west of us. And most of the fighting is along the Great Lakes."

"Well, I think it's disgraceful. None of the best Albany people are venturing out there. Nor are they the least bit interested in the war. A good many say it's all the same to them if the British win."

"I daresay a good many *want* the British to win," Alva said, tight-lipped. "The Federalists are afraid a war with Britain will be the ruination of their shipping trade. It's a wonder that President Madison managed to declare war, as much opposition as there is to it." Alva cast a reassuring look at his wife as if to say, *Don't worry, I'll keep my temper.* However, his voice had an edge as he added, "Some men of wealth and position certainly support us."

Mrs. Brock's pink cheeks were growing pinker and her eyes snapped. "Well, it's all beyond me. We beat the British back in Washington's time, didn't we? Why fight them again?"

"Because that's the problem. We beat the British during the Revolution, but they still have troops in American territory along the Great Lakes. We're still being treated like a colony," Alva said more heatedly, "and we have to win the respect of other nations."

Mrs. Brock huffed and fumed, but turned her attention to her daughter.

By the end of November everything was ready for Ruth's trip back east. The days were growing shorter, the nights colder, and it was important that they start before winter. Mrs. Brock had brought a new blue woolen dress for Ruth to wear. It was warm and soft and city-looking, with tiny buttons up the front. "I had it cut and made up quickly to your old measure, but of course you've gone thinner." She glanced at Alva, and Jessica felt her anger rising, although her father remained calm. "No matter," Mrs. Brock continued briskly, "we can have others made when we get home." She had left presents for Jessica and Linus too, lengths of dress goods and shirting, "because I just couldn't *guess* how big you had gotten." Then she had added, as if it were something not quite respectable, "I suppose you can sew, Jessica. Now do make them up, won't you, so you don't go around looking like such a scarecrow." But Jessica put the things away in the chest that stood at the foot of her bed in the loft. She had no heart for such trifles now.

At the last minute a flood of worries overtook Ruth, and with her small valise packed and the carriage waiting, she turned back anxiously. "There's plenty of candles, but when your father butchers the hog, Linus, you must be sure to help him, and Jessica, you should ask someone to come and help with the meat. You'll want to salt down most of it, and you must be *sure* to use enough salt. Widow Cosgrove might be willing to lend a hand—"

"Of course she will," Alva interrupted smoothly, ignoring the old lady's look of distaste at this talk of hogs. "And she'll be right there to help Jessie with anything else that comes up, too, so don't worry about us. We'll be fine."

"But I know I've forgotten so many things," Ruth said, suddenly close to tears, looking slender and beautiful in the new blue dress.

Alva put his arms around her and said, "Now, that will be enough of that, my girl. All we want is for you to come back fit and strong. We'll be counting the days."

She hugged them all and then left at last. It was a chilly gray day, and Jessica watched and waved

Chapter 2

JESSICA HAD BEEN dreading Christmas but keeping her dread to herself. It had been over two weeks—a long, lonely time that seemed to drag on endlessly—since her mother had gone, and Jessica could muster none of her usual Christmas excitement. She suspected that both Linus and her father were feeling the same way. Then one morning Alva Parish said, "As long as the weather holds, why don't we walk to church on Christmas day? Snow's packed down in the track and we've all got new boots to wear."

Jessica went on kneading bread dough and tried for an enthusiasm she wasn't really feeling. "Why, that'd be real nice. And I'll cook something special." Linus had brought down a deer after the first snow. They could have venison and perhaps potatoes baked in the low coals of a banked fire. And it would be nice to try out her new shoes. They'd been made up by Solomon Justice, the traveling bootmaker, earlier in December; soft as butter, the soles held to the uppers by maple pegs. She didn't take any real joy in them, though, as she would have if her mother'd been home.

Still, she smiled at her father and he smiled back, each pretending for the other's benefit that things were fine and life was going on as usual.

"It's a whole week away," Alva said thoughtfully. "Wouldn't that be time enough for you to make up a new dress out of the goods your grandmother brought?"

Jessica had given scarcely a thought to the cloth lying in the chest up in the loft. It was too painful a reminder of her mother's leaving. Also, she couldn't have real pleasure in anything that came from her grandmother's hand. But her last new dress really had been before the Great Flood, as her father always put it. Her wrists were hanging out of her old dress, and it was growing snug across the bosom.

"Maybe I could. And there's broadcloth, too. I could make shirts for you and Linus."

"Oh, Jess, Linus and I don't need to be beautiful."

"Well, you're going to be anyway."

For the next few days the house was a ferment of cutting and patterns, of scraps, threads, and lint as Jessica cut and seamed two shirts out of the fine broadcloth. Her mother had taught her to sew as soon as she was big enough to hold a needle, in spite of Grandmother Brock's disapproval. "Why spend time teaching her to do something that others can easily do for you?" she had asked. And Ruth had answered pleasantly, "When we live on our farm we'll be sewing all our own clothes, and I want Jessica to be able to help me." Jessica had beamed with pride at being so important, and she had taken extra care to be sure that her seams were straight and even.

When the shirts were done, she turned to the rose-colored wool. She carefully laid out her pattern, determined not to waste an inch of the cloth, and at night she sat up late, burning candles recklessly as she sewed and resewed, reinforcing seams and making buttonholes. Her father, who always counseled economy in the use of candles, made no objection, as if he knew how important this was—for Jessica and indeed for all of them, to lift their spirits.

Christmas morning those spirits plummeted when she opened the door to look out and saw that the day was gray, overcast, and threatening. Her father, leaning against the wind as he walked in from the barn, still looked cheerful.

"Do you think there'll be snow?" she asked anxiously. "Can we still walk to town?"

"Might be a storm building, but I judge it'll hold off awhile. Yes indeed, we're going. What's a little snow, anyway?"

"Oh, good." Jessica felt weak with relief. And probably that was another sin to her discredit, she admitted, wanting so much to be seen in the new rose-colored dress.

Chapter 3

"I'M WORRIED ABOUT Floss," Jessica said as they started out. "She wasn't in the house—I looked everywhere for her."

"She'll be fine," her father assured her. "Cats know how to find shelter. Likely she's in the barn."

"Yes, likely." It was only a small pinprick of worry anyway, and Jessica was sure her father was right.

They were all dressed warmly in their sheepskin coats and mufflers, their shoes well greased against the cold and wet. Under Jessica's coat was the new dress of rose wool, soft and luxurious, which Alva had praised extravagantly. "And these shirts! Why, you couldn't get better at a big city outfitter. Just look at your brother—he hasn't been so well turned out since he was baptized."

"Thanks, Jess," Linus said unexpectedly. "It's a real

fine shirt." He held out something. "This is for you."
He blushed as he handed it to her. It was a cooking
spoon he'd whittled, and even though a new cooking
spoon was hardly a gift to make her spirits soar, Jessica was touched at the work he'd put into it and
praised it highly. "I don't know as I ever saw finer,"
she said. Linus blushed to the roots of his red hair.
He was as tall as his father now and his shoulders
filled the doorway when he entered the house.

Her father had a gift for her, too, a rolled-up bundle
of white paper tied with a scrap of yarn—a wealth of
clean white sheets to write on. He must have traded
dear for that at the store, she thought. Paper was
hard to come by, even in a big city like Albany, and
people usually wrote on both sides and then went
back and wrote diagonally, crosshatching to get more
words on.

"We can write letters to Mother," she said.

"Yes, we can, but save some of it for yourself. Might
be you'd like to keep a journal or write down some of
your thoughts," Alva said. It was like her father to
suggest that, Jessica thought.

Now, walking along the rutted wagon track toward
the village, Alva began to hum and then to sing, and
Linus and Jessica joined in, the three of them striding
along singing old sweet hymns that echoed across the
icy river on their right and through the frozen
meadows.

Halfway to town they were joined by the Widow
Cosgrove and her two boys, Asa and Leander. The
widow, who was inclined to be grimy and more than
a little untidy, was today wearing her late husband's
greatcoat from the Revolution. A large woolen scarf

was tied around her head, and her hair, streaked with gray, hung from under it in a loose, careless braid. In warm weather her feet were always bare and seldom washed, but today they were encased in stout boots that Jessica thought might also have belonged to her husband.

"Merry Christmas, Mrs. Cosgrove," Jessica said. There was no one she'd rather have run into, even though she knew the widow's quick tongue and unstylish habits rubbed some people the wrong way. Mrs. Stillwater, the storekeeper's proud wife, always frowned with annoyance when she saw her enter the store. But Jessica's parents said the widow was a true Christian, "running that farm and bringing up her boys in godly ways." Jessica enjoyed her company.

"Happy Christmas, dearie," the widow sang out. "And just what I was hoping, that I'd run into the Parishes. Thought if I was to meet up with you, you could read me this letter from Eager. The boys and me, we made out some of it, but we couldn't get the whole sense of it."

Jessica, who knew the oldest Cosgrove boy was with the army to westward, took the smudged and much-handled letter and read aloud as they walked.

"It starts, 'November twenty-fifth, 1813.' Then it says, 'My dear Mother, I am well here with the army and hope all at home are same. Today things are quiet, but there has been some shooting. The American troops won a big victory on Lake Erie in September when Perry destroyed the British fleet. Then came other battles nearby, although our regiment was not involved. We eat not so much as home and not so well as your cooking, but I don't complain, as

14

there are many as has it worst. I hope you and brothers got the harvest in safe. Your loving and obedient son, Eager Cosgrove.' "

The widow didn't speak at once, and Alva said, "A very fine boy, Mrs. Cosgrove. You must be proud of him."

The widow swallowed and found her voice. "Thank you, neighbor Parish. Indeed I am. We surely miss him, but Asa and Leander do right well. Asa's seven now and Leander's going for twelve. Dearie, while we're walking along, why don't you just read that to me again?"

No regular church had been built yet in the village, so services were held in Barzilla Moon's turning shop. It was a two-story building, full of freshly-cut wood and sawdust from the furniture Barzilla built. Services were held on the second floor, and there were always plenty of unsold or half-finished chairs, benches, and stools to sit on. Today there was a good crowd, and the Parishes and Cosgroves lined up together on two long benches with straight backs. Mr. and Mrs. Stillwater from the general store were there, Mrs. Stillwater looking large and grand in dark red silk. Her whalebone stays creaked and the red silk rustled as she walked. Their stout, moon-faced son, Artemas, was with them. Jessica felt his eyes sliding over her as surely as if he were touching her with his pudgy hands. She shuddered slightly and kept her own eyes straight ahead. She couldn't abide Artemas, who never seemed to do any work, but went out every day with his rifle to shoot the woods creatures. Skinny Miss Ida Tate, the dressmaker, sat with them. She and Mrs. Stillwater were known to spend hours together in Miss Ida's thread-strewn little parlor, gossiping and eating cakes.

The minister, Pastor Baldwin, and his wife greeted Jessica and the rest of them warmly, and Mrs. Baldwin held Jessica's hand as she said how sorry she was that her mother had to be absent from the family and that Jessica wouldn't be in school. "But you'll manage, won't you? Of course you will. The Lord gives strength." Then she turned to her husband. "Aaron, we must visit the Parishes very soon. Let us *make* time."

"You'd be most welcome," Jessica said, thinking that when Mrs. Baldwin got that firm tone in her voice, it was likely they would come.

They all enjoyed the service, and the Widow Cosgrove sang the hymns louder than anyone. Jessica had never seen anyone enjoy church more. Mrs. Stillwater shot several disapproving looks in her direction.

Then it was over and Jessica waited outside while her father and Linus spoke to Moses Stillwater. "Any news from the west?" Alva asked. Anyone who traveled through the town stopped at Stillwater's store, and Moses knew more than most about the fighting.

Moses stroked his cheek thoughtfully. He greatly enjoyed being the center of attention and the main source of information for the town. "Well, I guess you heard Fort Niagara fell to the British."

Alva nodded solemnly. "Is that so? That seems to have happened mighty fast. Fort Niagara was General van Schoyk's command, wasn't it?"

Moses said that it was and added, "Just seems to be the way things are going right now."

Alva looked at him worriedly. "I don't like the sound of it, so sudden and all." He pulled at his beard. "Especially coming right on the heels of the big naval victory on Lake Erie. Makes you wonder how things could turn against us so fast."

"That seems to be the way of the war," Moses said. "First one side, then the other gets the upper hand."

Alva looked down and shook his head. As the two men continued to talk, Jessica's mind drifted back to the service, and she thought she felt a little more Christmas spirit for having come to church. If only her mother were here . . .

"Merry Christmas, Jessica."

She whirled around, startled. "Oh! Merry Christmas, Artemas." She swallowed her distaste and searched for her newly found Christmas spirit. "Lovely service, wasn't it?"

"Indeed. And you're looking lovely yourself. That's a new dress, isn't it?"

He stared intently at her, and Jessica could feel herself perspiring in the freezing temperature.

"I . . . yes . . . Grandmother Brock brought me some goods from Albany and I . . ."

"You about ready, Jess?" her father called, looking at Artemas.

Thankful for a means of escape, she bid a hasty farewell to Artemas, and the Parishes and the Cosgroves headed home along the track. The wind was stronger and a small spitting snow had started up. After they parted from the Cosgroves they walked single file, Alva first, then Jessica, then Linus. Jessica

17

scolded herself for letting Artemas make her so uncomfortable. *Don't pay him any mind* was what her mother would have said. Jessica found she could finally think of her mother without the dreadful pangs of loneliness. The last few weeks, the time since her mother had left, began at last to drop away from her. *It will be all right after all,* she told herself. *Reverend Mr. Baldwin always says when one door closes, another opens.*

Even the dark and empty house failed to daunt her. She lit candles and stirred up the fire, moved the potatoes to one side to stay hot, and stirred the stew she had left warming on the hob, the iron shelf in the fireplace. Then she took out the good linen cloth and the china plates her mother had carried west from Albany, and while her father and brother took care of the chores in the barn, she set the table for their Christmas dinner.

When Linus came bursting in the door moments later there was a big smile on his face. "Jess! Come out to the barn and see what's happened!" His red hair flared around his head.

Jessica thought it must surely be a good thing, judging by the smile on his face. She grabbed her coat and followed him out into the snow.

"Oh, how wonderful," she whispered as Linus and Alva stood back from the cow's stall, where old Bess was munching with loud contentment. In the corner of the stall was Floss, the orange cat, with a litter of four new kittens. Jessica knelt down in the straw and stroked Floss's head with her finger. "What a clever girl—to pick today to give us all such a nice present."

She stood up and looked around. "I'll find a basket to carry them in. We can let them sleep by the fire."

"Now wait, wait." Alva put out a hand to stop her. "Floss picked this spot because it suited her, and she was smart enough to know Bess would supply some heat, too. You just leave her be."

"Are you sure?"

"Sure as salvation. Now let's get in before the storm gets any worse. Linus, pour a little of that milk out for Floss."

Inside, the fire was blazing up and the smell of food was in the air. The table looked festive with the china dishes laid out instead of the everyday pewter ones. It would be a good day to write another letter to Albany, Jessica decided, to tell her mother about going to church, seeing friends, finding the kittens. And this letter would be on the new clean paper her father had given her. She put the food on the table and the three of them sat and bowed their heads in the firelight as Alva said grace.

Chapter 4

IN THE DARKNESS Jessica woke up suddenly. The wind was still shrieking around the house, but that wasn't what had roused her. Something was troubling about the night. Something was nagging at her. Her mind skittered this way and that, trying to lay hold of what it was. Then she remembered: Floss and the new kittens. Could they really survive a night like this in the barn? Her father had assured her they'd be all right, but that wind had an icy sound. Supposing the temperature had dropped suddenly? Might she not find their small bodies frozen stiff by morning? For several minutes she lay there worrying. At last she knew she was going to have to do something about it, whether it was wise or not.

She pushed back the covers and slipped into her

heavy moccasins, then climbed down the ladder in the cold dark. She went to the fireplace, lit a candle from the low coals, and stuck it in the metal lantern that gave off only a tiny light through the holes pricked in it. Then she reached for her coat on its nail by the door, found her father's instead, and put it on. It was long and heavy, with the fleece turned to the inside. She threw the bolt on the door and held her breath as she stepped outside.

The wind and snow struck her like a blow and almost grabbed the lantern out of her hand. She hung on to it tightly, grateful that it stayed lit, even though the light it gave was so feeble. She put her head down and made her way toward the barn. It was only fifty or sixty feet from the house, and in good weather she could cover the distance in no time. Now she had to fight the wind for every step, holding Alva's coat around her and feeling the snow creeping over her moccasins. When she got there she reached up to slide open the bolt, but the door was not bolted. Jessica felt a sharp thrust of fear. How could that be? Linus had been the last to leave. Could he have neglected to bolt the door? If so, she'd give him the rough side of her tongue and no mistake. It would be no trick at all for a clever fox or wolf to work the door open, and it was only luck that it hadn't swung wide in the freezing wind.

She opened the door and stepped inside, closing it behind her and holding the lantern high. The pinpricks of light helped hardly at all, but she knew her way to Bess's stall. She looked around her as she walked, a little nervous now that the thought of a wolf had occurred to her. Everything was quiet. She could smell the sweet heavy scent of Buck and Bright, the oxen, and there was Bess's half-grown calf, and the chickens roosting on the barn loft ladder. She felt her way slowly, hearing Bess's steady breathing. When she reached the stall she shone her light down into it. Bess, lying in the straw, turned her big head as if to inquire what she was doing there in the middle of the night. Floss and the kittens were nestled close to her in a contented heap. Jessica let out her breath with relief, feeling foolish and realizing that, as usual, her father had known exactly what he was talking about. She turned to leave.

It was right then, in that moment of turning, that something came to her. Linus, she thought. He was as pesky as most brothers, all right, but he wasn't careless about the stock. Linus would never have left the barn unbolted. Someone else had lifted that bolt. And not an animal, either—not a fox or a wolf. A person. And whoever it was—Jessica knew it with a sudden chill certainty—that person was in here right now with her. She stood still, holding up her lantern; her trembling made its light wobble in the cold dark. She could still smell the fragrance of the hay, feel the animals around her, but something else was there, too. Someone. She took a cautious step toward the door, trying to judge where the person might be. Then there was movement and a brush of sound between her and the door. She heard breathing that was not from the oxen or Bess. A human sound, throaty, almost a sob. Her fingers tightened on the lantern. Its feeble light picked out the figure of a man crouching in the shadows against the wall. He was staring at her.

Jessica stared back at him, but her mind was working desperately. Would they hear her in the house if she yelled? Not likely, over the storm. Who could he be? A deserter from the militia, maybe? She could tell he wasn't an Indian, but she'd heard plenty of talk about deserters. He was leaning against the wall as if he needed it for support. His knees were slightly bent so that he was almost crouching. It gave him a tired, spent look. Studying him, Jessica realized that he was a boy, not a man. Pretty near grown, maybe as old as Linus. But still a boy. It gave her some courage.

She took a firm step toward the door as if to march right past him, but at once he pushed himself upright and moved toward her. She saw something gleam in his hand.

A boy, all right. But he was carrying a knife.

She heard again the small sound that was like a sob. He was breathing hard, as if he'd been running, and with each breath came the little catch. He looked worn out, tired, cold. Probably hungry, too, she thought. But still he hung on to that knife.

She gripped the lantern tightly and demanded, "What are you doing in our barn? Where'd you come from?"

He didn't answer, just stood there looking at her.

"Are we going to stand here freezing?"

He didn't move, although she thought that the hand holding the knife tightened some.

"Who are you, anyway?" She could feel the cold

creeping up her legs. The boy was even less warmly dressed than she was. His coat was of wool rather than sheepskin or fur, and only a short coat at that. His britches were of cloth, too, not the buckskins that Alva and Linus wore. His dark hair had come loose from its tie and hung in a tangle about his shoulders. Dirt and grime smeared much of his face, but his eyes shone brightly, wild and scared.

Jessica had seen animals with the same wild look about them. *There's two ways to manage scared animals,* Alva always said. *Gentle 'em along first, but if that doesn't work, you have to take charge. Don't back down or let on you're scared.*

"You look real cold and hungry," Jessica said quietly. "I've got some good deer meat left in the kettle. Why don't you come along to the house and warm up?"

She took two cautious steps toward the door. In an instant he was beside her. One cold hand, surprisingly strong, closed around her wrist, and the knife flashed near her. She felt sudden terror, and on the heels of it a flare of anger.

"Now you look here," she said hotly. "You leave go my wrist and put that thing away. If you want to stay out here in the cold, you can stay. But I'm going inside and I'm bolting that barn door after me. So just make up your mind."

Standing this close to him, she could see that what she had taken for dirt on his face looked more like dried blood. There were bruises around his eyes and along one cheek. Her heart was thumping so hard it hurt. She wrenched her arm away from him and marched toward the door. Opening the door, she paused and looked back. He was standing where she'd left him. Bess gave a loud moo of complaint as icy cold whistled into the barn.

"Well?"

He followed after her slowly, still holding the knife.

Chapter 5

JESSICA TRIED NOT to think about the knife as she replaced the bolt on the barn door and led the way back toward the cabin, but her knees were turning limp with fear. The wind whirled and howled around them. Snow struck her face, and her feet floundered where drifts had blown across the path. Over the noise of the night and the pounding of her own heart, she could hear the steady pace of his footsteps behind her. She reached the cabin door and wrenched it open. When she stepped inside, he hesitated.

"Hurry up!" she said. "You'll have the whole place freezing."

He stepped over the threshold cautiously. Jessica closed the door and threw the bolt. The sound was loud in the still house, and almost at once Alva stood in the bedroom doorway. Jessica could just make him out in the dimness, standing in his warm nightshirt and cap, holding his rifle.

"Father—Pa—" she said in a voice that turned small as her courage dissolved.

"Who's that with you?" Alva demanded loudly. Up overhead she could hear Linus stirring awake.

"I went to the barn to see Floss and the kittens, Pa. And he was there. I don't know who he is."

There was a rushing and stumbling as Linus scrambled down the ladder from the loft. Sleepy and bewildered, he lunged across the cabin, seized the boy's arm, and bent it around behind him. The knife clattered to the floor.

"Lookit that, Pa!" he shouted. "He had a knife."

"Keep hold on him, Linus. Jessie, stir that fire."

Jessica put her lantern down, moved to the fire-place, and threw on a fresh log. Sparks flared up and flames rose. The light in the room grew brighter. Alva moved across to where Linus held the boy.

"In the barn? You found him in the barn?"

"Yes, hiding in there." Jessica had some trouble keeping her voice steady.

"And you fetched him back here by yourself?" A number of emotions were mixed in Alva's voice: disapproval, fear, admiration.

"I don't exactly know who fetched who."

"Well, by jiminy." Alva confronted the boy. "Who are you anyway, young man? What're you doing here this time of night?"

The boy didn't answer.

"I couldn't get a word out of him," Jessica said.

"Reckon he's a deserter, Pa?" Linus asked.

Alva Parish scanned the boy's face, the dried blood,

27

the bruises, the swollen eyes. "He's no deserter. He's not old enough for the militia. I don't think he's any older'n you are, Linus. Ease up on him a little."

Linus relaxed his hold on the boy's arm. Alva bent down and picked up the knife, then put both knife and rifle on the table. He turned back. "Now lookit here, son, you might just as well tell us right now—"

But the boy's legs bent and sagged as his whole body crumpled and sank to the floor. It was as if he had fallen asleep standing up. Jessica let out a little cry. Alva bent over, lifted him, and carried him to the fire, which was blazing up smartly now.

"Put a quilt down for him, Jessie," he ordered.

Jessica ran to the bedroom for one and spread it on the hearth. Alva gently lowered the boy's limp body onto it. Linus came over to look.

"What is it, Pa? What's the matter with him?"

Alva ran his hands over the boy, feeling his arms and legs. Then he pushed back the tangle of dark hair. "He's been hurt. Look there."

Linus and Jessica leaned over. Where Alva's hand had pushed back the hair, they could see that blood had dried and matted it. Alva touched the spot gently. "Swelled up and bloody. He's taken a good blow there. Jessie, fetch Mother's sewing scissors. We'll cut away some of the hair and clean that up. Need cloths and some warm water, too."

Jessica dashed back to the bedroom for her mother's scissors and bag of scraps. Linus brought warm water from the hob. Both of them moved quickly, hearing the urgency in Alva's voice.

In a minute he was snipping away hair and washing the wound while Linus stood by with a candle for extra light and Jessica began tearing linen into strips.

She looked down at the boy's sleeping face and whispered to her father, "Is it real bad? Is he going to die, do you think?"

"Well, it's bad enough." Alva worked calmly, but he wasn't wasting any time, she noticed. "We'll do the best we can and leave it in the Lord's hands. He's skin and bones and near froze, but once he's rested and fed, he might pick up."

"That's an ugly wound," Linus observed.

" 'Tis for a fact."

"Why do you reckon he didn't speak to us?"

"Oh, just too tuckered out, maybe, or scared."

"Maybe he doesn't understand English." Jessica handed her father a fresh cloth. "Sometimes there's people from foreign parts come out this way to settle."

"Could be that. But I had the notion he understood what we were saying. Likely once he's slept a little he'll talk to us. Now, Jessie, fold some of that cloth into a thick pad to put over the wound and we'll tie it up snug. Then you can bring a pillow and another quilt and we'll make a bed for him right here where he can warm all through."

The boy stirred and moaned and his eyelids fluttered as they fixed the bed for him, but he didn't really wake. Jessica brought him water in a gourd and he drank it without opening his eyes. Then Alva lowered him onto the pillow and they covered him warmly. Lying there with the white bandage wrapped around his head, he looked suddenly frail and near death. His breathing was fast and irregular and his face looked feverish. Remembering how angry and scared she'd been in the barn, Jessica thought that the boy now seemed like a different stranger, this one lost and hurt and not in any way terrifying.

"Reckon he might die at that, mightn't he, Pa?" she whispered.

"Well, he might." Alva looked sober. "I'll sit with him for a little bit. You and Linus go along to bed."

She started to say she'd sit up too, but then decided against it. It was obvious her father didn't want her to, and she guessed that, like her, he was thinking death might overtake the boy in the night.

She followed Linus up the ladder and crept over to her side of the loft, climbing in between icy cold sheets and pulling the covers up. Wind was still keening around the cabin. She heard Linus's breathing deepen as he dropped into sleep. She heard the unfamiliar crackling sound of the fire—unfamiliar because a fire was never built up like that at night—and now and then the odd rasping sound of the boy's breathing, rapid and unrelaxed. Presently she heard her father's voice, but it was low and she had to strain to hear.

"There now. That fire feels pretty good, I reckon. You just give up and sleep. No call to be scared here. Ain't anybody going to do anything to you." He spoke soothingly, the way Jessica had heard him speak to Buck and Bright when the oxen stumbled or shied at a woodchuck. For a long time she lay awake and thought how she would write all this down in her journal tomorrow while it was fresh in her mind. At last the warmth crept into the chilly bed and she slept.

*   *   *

The first thing she saw when she woke was the moving pattern of firelight on the roof boards overhead. She hadn't a notion what time it was. It might be morning, but with all the windows shuttered she couldn't tell. Then she remembered the strange boy. Was he still alive? She grabbed her clothes from the upended keg where she'd left them and dressed under the quilt, in her own nest of warmth. It was awkward, but she was used to it. She pulled on her heavy stockings, yanked her woolen petticoat and gray homespun dress on, and then came out and sat on the edge of the straw tick to do her buttons and brush her hair. She loosened her hair, brushed it and rebraided it, and then put a shawl around her, tying the two ends behind her to keep them out of her way. She shoved her feet into her moccasins and glanced across the loft at her brother's bed. Linus was still asleep. She smoothed her own covers then, taking out the soapstone bed warmer that had long since gone cold. She was still afraid to look down below. At last she crept fearfully to the edge and peered over. Alva was sitting about where she'd left him, a heavy shawl around his shoulders, his trousers pulled on over his nightshirt.

He glanced up and caught her eye. "Come take a look," he said softly. "Sleeping like one of Floss's kittens."

Jessica hurried over to the ladder and scrambled down backward, excitement bounding inside her. Maybe he was going to live after all. She didn't know him from Adam, but even so, she felt some connection with him, since she'd been the one to find him.

She tiptoed to the hearth and looked over her father's shoulder.

31

Chapter

6

"I'LL BE BACK by midday," Alva said. "I don't intend to tarry any."

It was five days after Christmas and they had just finished their breakfast of bacon and johnnycake. Alva drank his hot tea and leaned over to pull on an extra pair of warm woolen stockings. Over them he put the heavy boots Solomon Justice had made.

Linus and Jessica walked to the door with him and he added in a low voice, "Somebody in the village might know who he belongs to. I'll talk to Moses Stillwater, Pastor Baldwin—one of them might know how to find his kin. There's been a good many people coming from the fighting, passing through these parts trying to make it to the east."

Linus and Jessica nodded and watched him set off across the snow toward the river path and the village.

The sun was bright enough to make them blink. Then they pushed the door shut against the cold and the cabin was dark again. It was the darkness Jessica disliked most about winter. Still, the fire was built up and snapping cheerfully. It gave enough light for most of the chores.

The stranger was sitting near the hearth on a low stool, his knees drawn up, his hands clasped loosely between them. He was about as tall as Linus, but more lean and spare. His head was bandaged and his eyes seemed to look far off, gazing into the distance. He still wore the cloth britches, but had put on an old woolen shirt of Linus's while Jessica soaked his bloody one in a bucket of water.

Jessica sat at the table and continued the journal entry she had started before Alva left for town. She dipped her quill in the ink and wrote. *He seems to understand what we say but he has not spoken to us as yet. Pa thinks he might be about Linus's age.* Linus sat down next to her and said, close to her ear, "Pa wants to snake some logs in from the woodlot. I might walk up there and look 'em over."

Jessica put her pen down firmly and turned to face her brother. "You'll do no such a thing! Leave me here with him? Don't you dare."

Linus gave her a surprised look but kept his voice low. "All he's done is sit there like that ever since he came back to himself. And Pa took his knife." Alva had stuck the knife into a log high up at the side of the fireplace, out of reach.

"I don't care—you're not leaving me alone with him. You stay right here till Pa gets back."

Linus rolled his eyes upward with a great show

of weariness. "I thought you were so excited about saving him."

"Well, I am. I want him to get well. But he acts so peculiar—never saying a word and looking far off like that."

"Oh, all right—"

There was a small noise from the hearth and they both turned. The boy had dropped to his knees and was scooping up some scattered ashes with the small fireplace shovel, dropping them into the iron ash bucket. Then he took the willow hearth broom and swept up. Linus rose and walked over to him.

"Well, that looks a sight better," he said. He dropped down on his haunches and went on talking quietly to the boy. "When that kettle's full of ashes and they're good and cold, we'll dump 'em over at the ashery. Get fourteen cents a bushel for 'em."

Jessica followed her brother and stood behind him. "One time we dumped them and they weren't all cold," she said. "Sparks set fire to a good barrel and burned it right up."

The boy didn't answer. He studied her face and then he looked at Linus. His eyes moved around the cabin curiously.

Jessica and Linus exchanged a glance and then, as if in agreement not to make too much of it, went about their work. Jessica began to clear the table, and Linus sat on another stool and began greasing his boots. Jessica washed dishes, wrung out the stranger's shirt, and hung it on a peg near the fireplace to dry. Then she swept and made things tidy. Linus, when he'd stretched the greasing job as far as

35

he could, put his rag away and began to whittle on a piece of maple.

Jessica, warm and mussed from housework, glared at her brother. "Linus, if you're going to sit there and whittle, you could just as easy be notching hoop-poles for Pa."

He glowered at her so hard all his freckles jumped out. Alva was an expert woodworker and always had wood seasoning in the barn. But Linus, who'd do any amount of backbreaking work if it was outdoors— plowing, seeding, harvesting, caring for the stock— hated indoor jobs something fearful, Jessica knew. Still, it was winter, and now was the time to do those jobs.

"Oh, I s'pose," he muttered. He got up and came over to her. "I got to go to the barn to get the poles, you know," he added under his breath.

" 'Tisn't all that far," she said practically. "You'll be right in sight all the time."

He grunted and reached for his coat. "Be sure to check on Floss and the kittens," she added as he left. Jessica stayed handy to the door while he was gone. When he returned he was dragging a bundle of poles—hickory and black ash saplings that he and Alva had cut near the river last spring. The poles had been soaked until they were soft, then pounded and split in two. Now they were ready to be notched and used to hold together the buckets and barrels Alva made to earn extra money. Jessica knew Linus hated notching barrel hoops.

He spread the poles out on the floor near the hearth and went to Alva's tool shelf for an extra-small, sharp woodworking knife. Jessica saw him hesitate briefly. She flew over to him.

"What are you going to do?" she asked in a fierce whisper.

"I got my own knife. This is for him. He can help me."

"You're going to put a knife in his hand?"

"You saw he wants to be busy. Man can't just sit idle day after day. Anyway, I don't think there's an ounce of fight left in him." He brushed past her. She saw him hesitate again, but only briefly, and then hand the knife to the boy.

"Looky here now. You could give me a hand with this. I have to make lock splicers at the ends of these poles. You cut in like this, see? Cut a little chunk right out. Then at the other end cut another one, only headed the opposite way. See how they fit together?"

The boy turned the knife in his hand and examined it. Then he leaned over and picked up one of the split poles, all his movements slow and cautious. For a moment he studied what Linus was doing, and finally he began to nick away at the wood. Jessica let her breath out with relief and unclenched her hands under her apron. She turned back to her own work.

Linus had caught and cleaned two fish the day before and hung them outside to freeze. She'd make fish soup, she decided. She fetched them in and cut up potatoes, carrots, and onions to throw into the pot along with a little salt pork for flavor. Then, as she was grasping the heavy iron kettle by its handle, ready to take it to the fire, she felt a slight brushing movement against her shoulder. She turned, and there was the boy standing behind her. She shrank back and shot a look at his hands to see if he was holding the knife. They were empty. As she stood there pressed rigidly against the table, he reached past her, picked up the heavy kettle, carried it to the fire, and hung it. Then he returned to the low stool and went on working with Linus.

"Thank you," Jessica said in a small voice.

Once the soup was bubbling, she decided to catch up on the spinning. Her mother's strength hadn't been up to it for a long time, except for a little flax she worked up on the small wheel. But wool had to be spun on the great wheel, and that was a sight harder. You had to stand and stride back and forth, managing the wheel with the right hand and holding the thread up high in the left, guiding it onto the spindle. Still, it was a job Jessica liked.

She took down rolls of carded wool, well greased to make it pliable, and began working with it, and soon there was a mixture of sounds in the cabin—the whir of the spinning wheel, her own footsteps pacing back and forth, the crackling of the fire, the hum of the simmering kettle, the nick and snap of the boys' knives as they whittled away at the hoops. And presently her brother's voice, talking in low tones to the stranger.

". . . have my own farm, that's what I really aim to do. Father says there's more land to the north and east, and this side of the river suits me fine. There ain't any better land in the state for wheat. That's what I'd raise, wheat. And with Lake Ontario to the north and Lake Erie to the west—why, there's a clear water route almost to Cleveland. With the West opening up, people are going to be needing flour. . . ."

Jessica turned slightly and peeked at the two boys. They were still working busily, one ruddy and freckled, the other dark-eyed and pale. The pile of completed hoops at the boy's side was almost twice as big as Linus's. She watched him making swift clean strokes and forming tidy hooks. She smiled a little and went on with her spinning.

Alva returned at midday, stamping and blowing with the cold. Jessica and Linus looked at him questioningly, but he gave a slight shake of his head as if to warn them not to ask. He put down a bundle he was carrying and removed his coat.

"Looks like you two have been mighty busy." He gestured to the notched hoop-poles. "We've got us a fast learner and a hard worker here, Linus."

Linus beamed and nodded, but the boy just looked at the floor. Alva went on, "And what do you think of this for luck? The very day I pick to walk into town is the day Moses Stillwater has the glass ready for me. Said it just arrived."

"The windows?" Jessica dropped her wool and ran to look.

Alva began untying the rope that secured the bundle. "Well, of course I've been waiting a long spell for these, but there I was without a cent on me or a single thing to trade. Moses said, 'Go ahead, take 'em anyway so's you can start putting 'em in. Pay me when you finish some sap buckets.'" He wrestled with the knot and it finally came loose. "Well, I don't like doing business on credit, but I surely wasn't going to say no—" The rope fell away and he picked up two windows and brought them to the table, holding them against the firelight to show them off. One had four panes; the other was large and heavy-looking, with six panes. The glass was wavy, and colors and patterns quavered and danced as the light came through it.

Jessica was holding her breath. "Oh, they're beautiful! Where will they go?"

"Small one's for the bedroom. Big one's going right there." Alva nodded toward the tightly shuttered opening next to the fireplace.

"When can we start?"

"Right away. And after we've done that, Linus and I'll split that white pine we've been seasoning—make a good floor for the bedroom, just like the one in this room."

"Mother won't believe her eyes when she comes back," Jessica said, and she thought her father looked pleased. She wondered if he was thinking about his wife back there in Albany in a grand house where glass windows weren't regarded as any great thing at all, and where all the floors were of wood. She hoped that if he was, it wasn't giving him doubts and worries.

"She's going to be real happy, Pa," Jessica assured him, and Linus had sense enough to chime in and agree.

The stranger, who'd been standing a little apart, looked from one excited face to the other, his expression curious and wondering. Alva glanced at him. "I sure do have a good winter's work cut out for me. Maybe I bit off more'n I can chew. All those sap buckets I'll need to pay for the windows, and then all the work around here. I could use another pair of hands right enough. You seem like a good worker. Maybe you'd stay with us a spell and help out, boy. Think maybe you could do that?"

The boy looked for a long time into Alva's face, then nodded slowly.

Alva picked up the windows and propped them against the wall in a corner where they wouldn't be jostled. "Well, then. That's settled. But you're going to have to have a name. How about Daniel? Good Bible name. And Daniel survived an ordeal. The Lord tried him and found him worthy. Daniel suit you all right?"

Once again the boy nodded, this time a little self-consciously. Jessica and Linus exchanged a look. It wasn't hard to tell that their father hadn't learned anything about him. The boy still had no name, no family, and no home, or Alva wouldn't be offering him all three.

Chapter 7

JESSICA, LINUS, AND their father sat near the hearth
talking in low tones. It was late—past their usual
time for bed—but they couldn't talk together until
Daniel, weary and spent-looking, climbed the loft ladder and turned in.

"It's all bad news," Alva said then. "Everything
from the west sounds bad."

Jessica frowned. "But we thought things were going
so well. The big victory on Lake Erie in the fall—"

"But the British hold Fort Niagara now. And
there's some strange business about that. Nobody
seems to know how they came to take it so quick and
easy, for it was well armed, well guarded, and there
was more troops only a short march away. Since then,
two more of our settlements were taken, Lewiston
and Black Rock."

"Forts?" Linus asked.

"No, but there was stores and supplies there, I daresay. Both towns sacked, burned down. The British had Indians fighting alongside them. A bad business all around."

Jessica shivered. "People killed, you mean? Settlers?"

Alva nodded. "We're safe enough here, Jessie," he added quickly to reassure her. "They're a good thirty miles west of us, farther down the Niagara River from the fort, and we've got no supplies nor arms. Nothing they'd bother coming this way for. But as far as learning about Daniel—" He hesitated. "I couldn't find out a thing. And the Lord knows I asked everybody. Pastor Baldwin helped me. He had a half dozen refugees from the burned-out settlements at his house overnight. Barzilla Moon put down mattresses for more at his shop. The whole countryside there's overrun with refugees. They're going back east on foot, on horseback, any way they can, along the ridge road. This boy, Daniel, was probably one of them—likely just lost his way after he got hurt."

"And not one of 'em could place him?"

"Nary a one. I described him as clear as could be, too."

The three of them thought about it. "Well, ain't a thing we can do about it tonight," Alva said at last, putting both hands on his knees and pushing himself up. "We'll keep trying, and so will Pastor Baldwin and Moses Stillwater. They'll put the word out. Here now, I almost forgot to give you this, Jessie." He drew something from his shirt pocket, under his woolen vest. "Widow Cosgrove left you a Christmas remembrance at the store. Daresay one of the boys made it."

It was a goose-quill pen, curved and slit, much finer than her old crow quill.

"It's beautiful," Jessica said. She was touched by the gift, but it wasn't enough to cheer her up tonight after Alva's news.

Linus put ashes on the fire to bank it for the night and Jessica lit a candle to take with her. Suddenly Alva said thoughtfully, "Pastor mentioned the hurt to the boy's head. Said perhaps it did something to his power of speech. Now, I haven't read as many books as Pastor has, for sure, but it just didn't seem reasonable to me. The power of speech lies on the tongue, doesn't it?"

" 'Twould seem so," Linus agreed.

"But yet I wonder." Alva shook his head, and Jessica could see him trying to straighten it out in his mind.

Linus and Daniel slept in the loft now, and Jessica in the bedroom. Alva said she was the woman of the house while her mother was away, and he'd brought a straw tick into the main room for himself. Secretly Jessica felt lonely and chilly in the bedroom. She missed the loft, where she could feel some heat from below, and she missed the comforting slope of the roof overhead. In her parents' big rope bedstead she felt overwhelmed by the lonely dark and it took her a long time to warm up at night despite her soapstone bed warmer and thick feather quilt. Tonight, though, she was struck with a thought that brought some comfort. When the new window was put in, she'd be able to look out at the moonlight last thing every night.

*   *   *

44

Alva was a great believer in patience working miracles. "Give Daniel time," he told Linus and Jessica. "Gentle him along same as you would breaking new young cattle to the yoke. Sooner or later he'll speak to us." They agreed, but to herself Jessica reflected that for once Alva didn't seem to have the right of it, for Daniel never spoke. He nodded or shook his head when a question was put to him, and he folded his hands and bowed when Alva prayed before meals. He even made a little bobbing motion with his head as if to thank her when she handed him his clean shirt or a pair of warm hose she'd darned. But he never said a word. When Alva tried to question him about his family or where he hailed from, his eyes took on a faraway look and it was as if Alva hadn't spoken at all.

During the weeks that followed, he worked hard, most of the time outside. The woolen coat he had been wearing when Jessica found him in the barn wasn't warm enough against the cold winter weather, and Alva had given him an old sheepskin coat and a pair of buckskin trousers that Linus had outgrown. Although Linus was broader in the shoulders than Daniel, the coat still strained some across the back, but it protected him better against the wind and cold than his cloth coat. Daniel quickly learned how to make sap buckets, water buckets, and oak firkins for butter. He learned to split the white pine and cedar, struggled at fitting the staves together and then pounding the wet hoops around them. When Alva saw how quick and capable he was, he taught him to rive shingles, splitting them off the seasoned block of cedar with the frow and then cutting them down still thinner with the razor-sharp drawing knife. In no time he and Linus between them were turning out four hundred shingles a day, which they stacked in the barn along with the buckets. Jessica knew how important his help was. Most farmers never had two coins to rub together, but a man with Alva's wood-working skills could afford the little extras that made life easier, like the new windows that now brought light into the cabin and cheered them all up.

Jessica moved her spinning wheel so she could stand in the light while she worked, and even though it was only pale winter sunshine, the warmth from it went right into her bones as she spun. Its light caught her hair and shimmered off the spindle. Once when she stood so, she happened to glance off to where Daniel was filling the woodbox and saw that he'd paused in his work and was watching her. He looked away quickly and color came into his face.

When the pile in the barn was big enough, the buckets, churns, and shingles were loaded onto a flat sledge so that Alva and Linus could take them over the snow into the village. Alva couldn't rest easy until he'd discharged the debt for the windows. This time nothing was said about Jessica's staying alone with Daniel all morning. Without realizing it, they'd come to think of Daniel as one of the family. The time slipped by quickly, with Jessica talking as she went about her chores.

"They call it the intermittent fever—that's what Mother had, and if it hadn't been for that, she'd never have gone back to Albany, for she loves the farm. We miss her something terrible, but she'll be home in the spring. We wrote her about you, Daniel, and I know she'll be happy you're here, especially the way you help Pa so much."

She paused, her blue apron floury from the biscuits she was mixing, and glanced at Daniel. He was sitting on the low stool again, mending a piece of harness, but now his hands grew still. He put down the piece of leather he was holding and strode out of the cabin, his face white and sober.

Jessica felt a sudden anxiety. What had she said to upset him? But in a few minutes he was back and seemed himself again. And then she realized it must have been because she was talking about her mother. Likely it made him think of his own mother, wherever she was. Jessica scolded herself. How could she have been so stupid?

She mentioned it to her father later, and he frowned and said, "I just wish we could get him out with folks a little more, but he seems scared as a rabbit every time I bring it up. Be a good idea for him to see people, and who knows, someone might recognize him."

"Well, sooner or later," Jessica said.

"And he's never smiled. Not once," Alva said.

"No, he hasn't, for a fact."

Alva pulled on his beard, as he always did when he was trying to put his thoughts in order. "His not speaking—well, we can't say about that, for we don't know. Maybe he never spoke. But for a boy not to smile—not ever—" He shook his head, as if it worried him.

Chapter

8

THEN IN FEBRUARY came a milder spell of weather, and the fresh wind brought the Widow Cosgrove out to their cabin for a visit. So like it or not, Daniel found himself face-to-face with a stranger. Alva and Linus had gone up to the woodlot with the oxen, and Daniel was to follow them as soon as he filled the woodbox for Jessica.

Despite her joy at having a visitor, Jessica shot a nervous look at Daniel, hoping he wouldn't bolt and run. "Mrs. Cosgrove, I'm so pleased you walked over." She helped the woman with her layers of wrappings, which today included the late Mr. Cosgrove's voluminous and slightly smelly bearskin coat. Heavy woolen stockings bulged over the tops of her high moccasins, and her head was wrapped in a tattery shawl.

"Hello, darlin'!" she shouted, embracing Jessica

warmly. "I just up and come when I saw the fine day. Here, I brought you some little things. Couple of jars of my raspberry preserves and a slab of that honey from the bee tree Leander found. Remember when he found that tree? And here's another thing." She held out something bulky. "Old coat useta be Eager's before he went in the military. I heard about the boy you've got with you—thought maybe he could use it. Here, son. Let's see how it fits. How do they call you— Dan'l, is it? Here, Dan'l. Slip 'er on."

Daniel, who had started to shrink back into the corner by the woodbox, stepped forward hesitantly and allowed the widow to yank the coat up over his arms. She slapped him smartly between the shoulder blades.

"There! Lookit that. If that ain't a good fit. My, but he's got broad shoulders. Fills it right in, and Eager must have two years' age on him. How's it feel, son— good and warm?" When no answer came, she went on cheerfully, "That's from my old flock of sheep— ones I useta have before I got the merinos. Barebellies, Mr. Cosgrove useta call 'em, and it's true, they wasn't any great amount of fleece to 'em. But what they was, on the backs, you know, was just as warm and thick—"

She paused, looking up into the boy's face, studying him with a kindly, curious look. She reached out and placed a hand on his arm. "Don't like to talk, eh, son? That's what I heard. Well, that ain't so terrible. Most of us do considerable more of it than we need to, me in particular. You look like a good boy to me, and I know boys pretty well. Why don't you and Jessie walk over to my place for a visit one day?"

He looked a little flustered, Jessica thought, but not really scared. She steered the widow over to the fire while Daniel edged out of the cabin, still wearing the coat.

"That was real kind of you, Mrs. Cosgrove," Jessica said. "That coat of Eager's fits him a sight better than Linus's old sheepskin. Now you sit right there and warm up. I'm going to make us some tea."

"Well, all right." The widow settled herself in a flurry of rags and wrappings. "But I won't just set. Hand me your knitting. I'll turn the heel of that stocking for you while we visit. My, but that's a fine-looking window. Lights the whole place up. I heard your father got glass. Well, now, what do you hear from your dear mama? Lots of surprises for her when she gets back, eh? New windows and the new boy and all."

"He's been a big help to us." Jessica felt her face grow warm as she reached up to the shelf for teacups. "Mother writes that she's pleased we have extra hands to help."

"I just wager she is," Mrs. Cosgrove said, eyeing her closely. "Artemas Stillwater's put it out all over that the boy's loony, but there ain't anybody I know pays much attention to Artemas—great lazy thing, takes after his mother. That boy's not anywheres near loony. Bright as a penny, he looks to me. . . ." The widow reached inside the folds of her coat and pulled out a tattered envelope. "I've gotten another letter from Eager. Would you read it to me, dearie?"

Jessica took the letter from her and began to read: " 'January first, 1814. Dear Mother and brothers, I am fine although anxious to be home again. I thought of you often over Christmas and the start of the new year. Things stay quiet here, but the news is that last October General William Henry Harrison overtook the British at Moraviantown—the battle of Thames, I heard them call it. A Shawnee chief named Tecumseh was killed there. There was plenty of rejoicing around our camp when we got the news. Some are worried that now that the British have defeated Napoleon in Europe, they will transfer more ships and troops to America. I am surely glad I wore my own coat when I went in the army, as many of the boys are still waiting for cloaks and blankets to be issued, and it's mighty cold to be without at this time of year. Your son, Eager Cosgrove.' "

It was midafternoon before the widow left, and Jessica watched her all the way out of sight as she strode across the frozen ground, a small figure in the flapping bearskin coat. The day was clouding up and turning colder. She turned back to the room and wondered at the strange feelings she'd had earlier as Mrs. Cosgrove was talking about Daniel. Just excitement over having a visitor, she told herself.

At supper that night, Jessica said, "I believe I'd like to pay the Cosgroves a visit one day when it's fine out."

Alva frowned. "I don't know, Jessie. It's a good three miles."

"That's not far. And I could cut through the woods. Walk it in an hour easy."

" 'Tisn't just that. But storms come up fast, and besides, I don't know how safe it is for a young girl." He didn't mention deserters or other vagrants who might be hiding in the woods, but Jessica knew what he was thinking.

"I didn't mean to go alone," she said, glancing across the table. "Daniel could go with me. Mrs. Cosgrove said he was welcome."

Alva looked at the boy in surprise. "That so, Daniel? You aim to go visiting, too?"

Daniel hesitated, his eyes going from Jessica to Alva. Then he gave a faint nod.

"Well . . ." Alva thought it over. "I guess then maybe if you were to pick a good day, 'twouldn't do any harm."

They had to wait some for a good day, however, for the mild weather turned to cold again and there was more snow. But at last the sun came out, and on a bright day, with the snow hard and squeaking underfoot, Jessica and Daniel set out for the Cosgrove farm. Daniel wore Eager's old coat and carried Alva's rifle, which Alva insisted on as a sensible precaution. Jessica carried under her coat a present for the widow— one of Floss's kittens. She knew it would be welcome, for the widow often remarked on how the mice plagued her, and now the kittens were old enough to leave their mother and drink from a saucer. Jessica picked the stoutest, strongest one. It had orange stripes and a neat white front and white forepaws.

They headed southeasterly over Alva's flat fields, but then the land rose slightly and woods appeared.

"We can cut through here," Jessica said. "It's a good bit shorter." She led the way, picking a path skillfully. She and her mother often walked this way in summer to visit the widow and she knew it by heart.

"My father and Mr. Cosgrove were the first settlers in these parts," she said over her shoulder. She felt nervous and fluttery. Not that she was scared of Daniel—just the opposite. She felt an odd and unaccustomed thrill at being in the silent countryside with him. But she couldn't seem to keep *herself* quiet. "They met on the way west from Albany and walked along together. Rest of us stayed back east with Grandmother Brock till he bought this farm and put up a cabin."

She hadn't talked this much since recitations in Mrs. Baldwin's class. She willed herself to be quiet as she waited for Daniel to catch up. He stopped when he reached her and lifted his hand to gently brush some snow from her hair. Jessica swallowed. "Pa and Mr. Cosgrove helped each other a good bit," she said quietly. "It was a whole year before he came back for us." Daniel stroked her hair lightly. "We lived with my grandmother in a big house painted white—"

Suddenly he pulled his hand back and raised a finger to his lips. He was frowning. Jessica started to ask a question, but he shook his head for her to be silent. Then she heard what he must have heard— the soft, stealthy sound of footsteps crunching over the snow somewhere nearby. She saw his hand tighten on the rifle. Her heart gave a thump of fear as the two of them stood in the stillness of the bare winter forest, listening to the steps coming closer and closer.

Chapter 9

JESSICA REACHED OUT and grabbed Daniel's free hand tightly, but only for a moment, because he pulled away and gripped the gun across his chest with both hands. Whoever it was was coming right behind them, probably in their footsteps.

"Do you think—" Jessica whispered, but he frowned and shook his head again for her to be silent. He gave her a push so that she was behind him and had to peer around him to see. Then a figure came in sight over a slight rise and through the trees. Jessica let her breath out with relief and stepped around Daniel.

"Good heavens, it's only Artemas Stillwater," she said. "He's Mr. Stillwater's son—they keep store in the village." She raised her voice. "Hello, Artemas." As always when she spoke to him, she found herself having to struggle for a pleasant tone.

"Afternoon, Jessica." Artemas's pale eyes moved sideways, sliding over Daniel but not taking any official notice of him. He was warmly bundled in a rich beaver coat, looking stouter than ever and carrying his rifle. "I was out hunting and I saw you leave home and cut over through the woods."

"You followed us all that way?" she blurted out, and then realized how angry it sounded. "I mean— you should've called out so we could walk along together." She thought her voice was giving her away. Walking anywhere with Artemas was the last thing she'd have wanted. She glanced at Daniel. His eyes had narrowed as he scrutinized Artemas, and she thought his mouth looked angry. The situation would have to be met head on.

"This is Daniel. He's staying with us."

Artemas gave Daniel a look that was like the first one, sliding and sidelong, without friendliness, not even acknowledging him. "I heard he's a dummy," he said.

Jessica's cheeks flamed with embarrassment. "Artemas, what an awful thing to say!"

Artemas shrugged. "I wonder your pa saw fit to let you walk out alone with him. And him carrying a rifle, too. I don't see as how he can be right in the head or he'd say something."

Jessica felt a red wave of anger sweep over her at the way he talked, as if Daniel weren't even there. "Now look here, Artemas," she began, but then she glanced at Daniel and saw how pale and tense he'd gone. Standing around talking was only going to make things worse. She grabbed his elbow. "Come on, Daniel, we'd best be getting along."

But Daniel shook off her hand and took a step toward Artemas, who was standing only a few feet away from them. Artemas, nervous and watchful, gave Daniel a shove. "We don't want your kind around here, dummy. And when Jessica's pa finds out what you've been up to behind his back, he'll help me run you out of here for sure."

Jessica felt her face turn scarlet, but just as she was about to make a sharp retort, Daniel lunged. Artemas took a nervous step backward and, as neatly as if it had been arranged by fate, a fallen log caught him behind the knees and threw him off balance. His carefully oiled rifle went flying out of his hand and into a heap of snow. He himself landed on his back with both feet kicking helplessly in the air. For an instant Jessica and Daniel just stared at him. Then she yanked at Daniel. "Come on," she said abruptly, forcing him to start walking along with her. Inside her coat, the kitten mewed and protested. She kept shooting glances at Daniel, seeing the anger in his eyes and the pinched look of his mouth. Not until they reached the widow's farm did he start to look like himself again.

The visit was a real success, at any rate. The widow was overjoyed with the kitten. Leander and Asa ran at once to fetch food for it, after which the kitten made itself at home, curling up before the fire and purring loudly.

"There ain't a thing you coulda fetched me that would've pleased me more," the widow said. She brought out all of Eager's letters for rereading, and they agreed the most recent one, dated February first, had a hopeful sound. The troops were toughening up,

Eager had said, and come warmer weather the tide would turn, he was sure of it. The widow included Daniel in all the conversation, not making any fuss when he didn't answer. Jessica said nothing about the incident in the woods, fearing it would only rouse Daniel's anger again. Then just as they were about to leave, the widow drew Jessica aside and whispered, "Maybe the boy can write. Ever think of that?"

Jessica shook her head. "He never made any move to. I suppose I just figured he couldn't."

The little woman shrugged. "Looks to me like the sort that might know writin'."

Jessica thought about it as they made their way back home, but decided she wouldn't bring up the subject yet. Daniel had had enough excitement for one day, going visiting and having a run-in with Artemas Stillwater.

Heavy gray clouds were building up as they reached their own log fence and climbed through it. Snowflakes began to fall, driven by a strong wind. Jessica saw her father standing before the doorway of the cabin, looking anxiously toward the southeast. She waved to him and he waved back. Then she and Daniel both began to run.

All through supper she thought of words and phrases that she could write in her journal later. She liked to keep track of special days that way. And today, she decided, was certainly special. She could still feel Daniel's hand on her hair as if he'd just brushed the snow away a moment ago. She stole glances at him during supper, but he kept his head bowed over his dish as if his food were a lesson he had to learn by tomorrow.

The most important thing came later, however, when they'd finished eating and were sitting by the fire. Alva asked about their visit to the widow, and because Jessica thought it would be wrong not to tell him, she described their encounter with Artemas.

Alva frowned and shook his head. "That boy's going to bring sorrow to his family yet," he said.

Linus was more direct. "Great no-account bully. Got what he deserved."

Jessica couldn't hold back a smile. "He looked like a fat beetle, with his legs waving in the air that way."

Linus hooted with laughter, and even Alva had to smile. Then they looked toward Daniel, who sat on the low stool whittling oak pegs for the new floor. Sensing their eyes on him, he looked up.

And then he grinned, too.

Chapter
10

THEY ALL STOOD watching Alva as he circled the big pine log and examined it from every angle. It was a cold, bright day in March with the ground almost free of snow. Finally he raised his heavy wooden beetle—the big maul used for log splitting—and came down with a crashing blow on the wedge he'd driven into the log. A clear, smooth board fell away, split off true and straight.

"Perfect!" Jessica shouted.

Alva examined the board. "You can't beat good old free-splitting white pine. Better'n you'll find at a mill."

After it had been sufficiently admired, Linus and Daniel picked up the board and carried it into the cabin while Alva began to insert more wedges for a second one.

"High time we got to this job," he said. "After this we'd best be sure all our tools are in good shape for the spring. Few more weeks, we'll be plowing."

They all helped lay the floor in the bedroom, and Jessica, when she went to bed that night smelling its sweet pine scent and looking out through the new window, thought how surprised her mother would be. Spring was only weeks away now, and that was when she'd be coming home, just as soon as the roads dried up.

Even after the floor was laid, however, Alva wasn't satisfied. There was still another thing he wanted for the room.

"A stove?" Jessica repeated.

Linus gave her a scornful look. "Did you never hear of a stove?"

Jessica ignored her brother. "But where would you find one?"

"Moses Stillwater has one in the store. Wants ten dollars for it, though."

"Ten dollars! But sap buckets bring only six cents apiece." Jessica was calculating rapidly.

Alva rubbed the back of his neck. "Can't do it with sap buckets. Not if we worked till victory and salvation. Have to figure some other way."

It was on his mind all week. Jessica could see how he paced and scowled and pulled his beard, trying to work it out. Finally he walked into the village and came back jubilant.

"I've got the answer." His eyes were full of excitement. "Tomorrow morning, boys, we'll go out to the woodlot for the other big pine. I've sold it."

No one quite understood. "How can you sell a tree?"

"Who'd you sell it to?"

"Man settled up north of here. Good land, right enough, for wheat, but flat, real flat, and not a tree on it, hardly. I met him in the store. He gave it out that he'd really admire to find some clear white pine, and what's more, he'd pay for it. So I said, well, what about ten dollars for a seasoned white pine big enough to floor your whole cabin and some left over for shingles, and he said done. We shook on it."

"Do we have to take it to his place?" Linus asked.

"That was part of the deal. But it's building up for more snow right now, so by tomorrow the ground ought to be covered. We'll hook up Buck and Bright and we'll be able to drag it there."

Jessica thought the new stove a wonder of an invention. It stood in the bedroom right up against the back of the main chimney, and Alva chipped away enough stone to make an opening for the pipe. They shoveled hot coals in, and then the little stove, which was only a square black box on curved legs, grew warm, and the whole room lost its winter chill.

She didn't know when she'd seen her father so pleased. To cover it up, he said gruffly, "Well, now that we've finished with all this foolishness, we'd best sharpen our tools and look over the plow—get ready for real work."

Jessica's eyes caught Daniel's and a spark of amusement passed between them, both of them recognizing that Alva didn't think it was foolishness at all.

Early in April there were heavy rains that washed away the snow and turned the dooryard into a slough, but nobody minded, for there was indoor work to be done. Between the barn and the house they stayed under cover while the rain pounded down on the tight roof shingles. Alva kept turning out kegs and barrels, working up to the last possible minute, letting the boys do most of the tool sharpening and harness mending. Only when it came to the plow did he take a hand, inspecting it carefully to be sure it was sound and the small bit of iron that protected the plowshare was tight and true.

Jessica mended and sewed, using up the last of the broadcloth on a shirt for Daniel in hopes they might be able to coax him out to church some Sunday when the mud began to dry. She darned stockings and put patches on the short gray britches and tow-cloth shirts Alva and the boys would be wearing for outdoor work in the spring. She finished her spinning and put the bundles of yarn away for dyeing or for trading at the store. She mended her own petticoats and stockings, knowing that once work started in earnest there'd be no more time for such things. She wished she had another length of goods for a dress, for the rose-colored wool would soon be too warm, and her only other dress, outside of the gray homespun she wore every day, was a blue one her mother had made her last year. She doubted it would fit anymore.

There were letters from Albany. *You would hardly believe how hale and strong I've become, resting lazily the whole winter through. Now I am so impatient to be home I cannot wait until the roads dry up.* And again, *I can picture just what you are all doing, especially if it's raining there as it is here. Mending tools, sharpening the axes. How I long to be with you! And how close and crowded the city seems to me.*

When they wrote back to her, they took turns composing their own messages. Once Jessica held out the goose quill to Daniel and said, "Want to add something? There's room."

But he put his hands behind his back and shook his head. So perhaps that was the answer to that, Jessica thought, remembering what the widow had said. Maybe he never had learned to write.

"I'll put in a message for you," she said. "I'll write, 'Our new friend Daniel sends warm greetings.' Will that do?"

He gave a hesitant nod, and as she wrote it his eyes followed the movement of the pen over the paper.

In her journal Jessica wrote, *Father is sure Daniel has never done farm work before, yet he has been so helpful to us. Linus says he has to be told how to do everything, but told only once. Which would seem to show, I think, that he really has a good mind and isn't in any way lacking in the head, for all that he can't speak.*

Then, at last, a Sunday came that was fine enough for walking to church, most of the mud dried and the sun strong and warm. Alva, brushing at his boots, called up to the loft, "Why don't you come along with us, Daniel?"

There was no answer, but Linus slid down the ladder a moment later and whispered, "He's coming."

Jessica, tying a shawl over last year's blue dress to hide how snug it was, looked up in surprise, and so did Alva. For there came Daniel, climbing down carefully and turning to face them. He was wearing his old jacket and britches—mended and pressed by Jessica—new stockings she'd knitted, and the shirt she'd made out of the last of the Albany goods. He'd filled out since Christmas, and his hair was neatly brushed and tied. It had grown back over the spot where he'd been wounded.

Jessica's breath caught in a little gasp as she looked at him. "My goodness, how fine you—" She blushed and rephrased it. "How fine all of you look."

"Well, let's go, let's go," Alva said, sounding impatient but pleased. "We're supposed to sing the Lord's praises, not our own."

Jessica and her father led the way into the village, with Linus and Daniel following. She could hear their footsteps behind her all the way, and she thought she could pick out which ones were Daniel's.

Chapter

11

THEY'D HARDLY ARRIVED at Barzilla Moon's shop before Jessica knew with dreadful certainty that there was going to be trouble. The air was still full of spring, the sun bright and warming, and the fine day had brought out a good number of worshippers. But there were the Stillwaters just ahead of them, climbing the stairs to the second floor, where services were held, and Artemas and his mother were greeting everyone, mingling and gossiping. Mrs. Stillwater was in dark green silk this time, and Miss Ida Tate, the dressmaker, trailed in her wake. Artemas was finely turned out in buff-colored trousers and a dark blue waistcoat. His buff-colored coat had blue turnings on the lapels and silver buttons that strained to hold it together over his stomach.

Jessica gave a quick, nervous glance at Daniel, but

at the same moment Pastor Baldwin came over to greet them. "I said to my wife, the Parishes would surely be here today," Pastor Baldwin said. "And you've brought your new friend." He put out a hand to touch Daniel's shoulder. "You are certainly most welcome, Daniel. Mrs. Baldwin!" he called to his wife. "Look who's come to services."

They'd all exchanged greetings and started to climb the stairs when the Cosgroves arrived. Mrs. Cosgrove sang out a loud halloo and caught up with them. She'd put aside her bearskin today but was still well wrapped in shawls and scarves, which trailed and flapped in her wake. "And look who come along," she sang out happily, slapping Daniel's shoulder. "Grand day for church, ain't it?" She leaned closer to him. "If you don't plan to sing, I'll sing loud enough for both of us." Daniel smiled at her, and she went on to describe how well the kitten was faring and how much bigger and stouter it was now. At the other side of the room, moving majestically in her green silk, Mrs. Stillwater eyed the widow and Daniel malevolently and nodded a cool greeting to Alva, Jessica, and Linus. Jessica wondered what version of their encounter in the woods Artemas had given her. Moses Stillwater, the storekeeper, trailed along behind his wife and son, but after a first low greeting didn't look toward the Parishes. Jessica guessed that he felt some small sense of embarrassment, for he and Alva had always been friends.

"Start plowing in another week or two, eh, neighbor Parish?" Mrs. Cosgrove said, settling down on the straight-backed bench.

Alva nodded. "There's life in that sun. I can feel it, even though the air's got a nip."

"And that warm weather'll bring your missus home, too."

"That's the day we're all waiting for, right enough."

Sunlight came in the unshuttered windows and the smell of cut lumber drifted up from downstairs as Pastor Baldwin began the service. Jessica's eyes took in Linus and Daniel, both so well turned out in their new shirts and cloth britches, and her father, tall and fine-looking in his Sunday best, his beard trimmed and brushed. She saw Alva's eyes wander to one side and fix on a little slat-back rocking chair that had been shoved off into a corner to make room for the worshippers. He caught her watching him and looked away quickly, as if mindful that it was the Sabbath. But Jessica wagered he was already figuring out a trade to propose to Barzilla for that chair, which would fit so well in the bedroom next to the new stove.

It was the best Sunday she could remember in a long time. She drank in Pastor Baldwin's words, said amen when he prayed, and when he called for a hymn, her own voice was at least as loud as the widow's. She cast one or two looks at the Stillwaters, but then tipped her chin up and resolved not to let Artemas or his mother upset her on such a fine day.

Pastor Baldwin pronounced a benediction on all of them—"old friends and new," he said, smiling at Daniel—and everyone got up to leave. People gathered in small groups to chat on their way out, and Jessica kept a sharp eye on the Stillwaters to make sure to stay out of their way. Pastor Baldwin and his wife had gone to the back near the stairway and were shaking hands as people left. Artemas, his parents, and Miss Ida Tate shoved along and were now between the Parishes and the stairs. Not only that, but they were lingering, Jessica noticed with dismay. Unless they hurried and left, her family would have to go right by them.

Suddenly she heard Artemas's voice, loud enough to be heard all over the room. "Oh, I could tell he was comin' for me, all right. Carryin' a rifle, too, so I just figured I'd step out of the way and avoid trouble."

"Artemas never looks for trouble," his mother chimed in, her round face a study in tremulous pride.

"Well, I sure didn't want to provoke him any. For all I knew, he might be aiming to harm Jessica. Don't any of us know the first thing about him, and what I felt was, he might not be all there, you know." Artemas tapped his own head significantly. "Never speaking a word to a soul. But then what he did was, he give me a shove. Tripped me up and threw me off balance. Well, shoot, I wasn't worried for myself, I was just thinkin' about that girl. It was her I wanted to protect." He glanced around at his listeners, looking pleased and proud.

Jessica caught her breath in an angry gasp. "That's not what happened," she blurted. She felt her father's hand tighten on her elbow before she could go on. "But Pa, he said—"

"Just move along," Alva whispered. "Don't you pay him any mind, Jessie." She saw that he was holding Daniel with his other hand.

Mrs. Stillwater put in worriedly, "Artemas was considerable shaken up. I told Mr. Stillwater so. Miss

68

Ida, what was that story you were telling me about some people who took in a stranger and the cabin burned right up one night with them in it? Over east of here, if I remember right. . . ."

Moses Stillwater's voice came in then, loud and overriding the others. "All right, folks—Artemas—let's move along here. I believe we're blocking the way." He shot Alva a look that might have been an apology; Jessica couldn't tell. In that instant the whole room grew quiet and it seemed as if all eyes turned toward the Parishes and Daniel. The store-keeper's family and Miss Ida shrank back as if to avoid contact with them.

Alva strode along briskly, looking neither right nor left but holding tight to both Jessica and Daniel. Jessica didn't dare look at Daniel's face, but she was holding back a powerful urge to kick Artemas in the shins as she went by.

"Bid you good day, Pastor, Mrs. Baldwin," Alva said calmly, and the poor minister, who surely had heard Artemas, could only thank them for coming and lay a hand gently on Daniel's arm. Widow Cosgrove and her boys were right behind them. "Hold on, neighbor Parish. We'll walk along with you," she called out, and Jessica turned just in time to see her direct a black look at Mrs. Stillwater—sharp as a cobbler's awl stabbing through boot leather, Jessica thought.

When they were outside in the sunshine, she looked timidly at Daniel, and his expression gave her a chill. His face had gone white and his eyes were narrowed to slits, his mouth drawn into a line so thin and angry that he seemed like a stranger again, just as he had on Christmas night in the barn.

Jessica walked along between her father and the widow, hearing them talk about crops and plowing, both avoiding any mention of what happened. Asa and Leander followed behind them, and several paces back Linus and Daniel walked together, Linus keeping up a quiet, one-sided conversation, reminding Daniel that there were some people—like Artemas— who weren't worth a pint of sour owl spit and never would be, and he didn't know of anybody this side of Lake Ontario who paid one ounce of attention to the fat bully. Another time, Jessica knew, her father would have reprimanded Linus for speaking so, but she guessed he either wasn't listening today or was purposely ignoring it, maybe because Linus was pretty much echoing his own opinions.

When she stole a look over her shoulder, though, she could see that all Linus's reassurances hadn't moved Daniel an inch. His face was still a study in cold fury, and when little Asa Cosgrove hopped over to him and grabbed his hand to walk along with him, he hardly looked at the boy, just marched straight ahead so that Asa had to run to keep up.

Their midday meal was waiting for them when they got home, for Jessica always set a pot of beans in the coals to cook slowly over Saturday night and Sunday morning. There was salt pork with them and molasses for their bread. All except Daniel ate hungrily. He poked at his plate and swallowed a mouthful or two, but then he pushed it away from him and got up so suddenly they all jumped as he strode across the cabin and went banging outside. Linus got up and made to follow him, but Alva called him back.

"Wait a little bit, Linus. Let him have some time to himself. He'll straighten out all right."

Jessica went to work clearing the table and washing dishes. Then calmly, because that was the way he was, Alva got out the Bible and read a few verses aloud from Ecclesiastes, a favorite of his—the part about how man "should make his soul enjoy good in his labor." Jessica guessed that was because spring plowing was just ahead. Then his voice got a little louder as he read, " 'I said in mine heart, God shall judge the righteous and the wicked: for there is a time there for every purpose and for every work.' "

She thought it was about as close as he would get to saying anything spiteful about Artemas.

After he closed the Bible he asked Jessica if she had taken note of the little rocking chair there at the turning shop. "I didn't want to talk trade on the Sabbath," he said, "but I might just speak to Barzilla this week and see how he's fixed for sap buckets and churns, see if he's of a mind to make a trade."

Jessica said she thought it was a fine idea. And then it seemed that they'd exhausted every subject, and the afternoon was wearing away. Daniel still hadn't come back. Linus said he'd go see about chores.

"I'll bet he's out in the barn," Jessica said. "I'll come with you. Maybe between us we can talk him around." She reached for her heavy shawl.

He was in the barn all right, but the minute she saw him, she knew it would take more than words. He was huddled against the wall in the very spot where she'd first seen him, sitting with his knees pulled up and his head resting wearily against the wall. Some of the fury had left his face, but it was dark and brooding now, as if turned inward on something they couldn't see. Two of the kittens, frisky and fat, darted at each other under Daniel's raised knees, but they might not have been there for all he was aware of them. He raised his eyes and looked at Jessica and Linus.

"Daniel—" Jessica's voice was low and timid. "Don't you want to come in now and have something to eat? You didn't take more than a mouthful before."

He looked away from her.

Linus tried to sound businesslike. "Might's well get on with chores, then."

Daniel pulled himself to his feet, took a bucket from its peg on the wall, and headed for Bess's stall.

Jessica exchanged a quick look with her brother, but Linus shook his head, and she turned to go back to the house. There hadn't been a spark of friendliness in the way Daniel looked at her, hardly even recognition. It was as if he'd turned back into a stranger.

Chapter
12

FROM THAT DAY on, Daniel went about his work the same as he always had, but there was a difference in the way he looked and acted. At night, Jessica wrote in her journal, *Daniel seems quieter, but I guess you can't really say that about someone who's never been anything but quiet.* She thought for a moment. It was more that his silence was heavier, darker. *He seems to be thinking private thoughts that weigh upon him,* she wrote, *and he shuts the rest of us out.* It made Jessica edgy to think that he might be angry enough at Artemas to do something foolish, like picking an open fight with him. Still, he'd shown no desire to go to the village on his own, so perhaps she was only looking for worries. *The hardest part is that he's so distant with me.* Once it was on paper she knew it bothered her more than anything. *He hardly looks at me, and it's been ages since we took a walk together. It's as if that business with Artemas wiped out everything that came before.* Jessica suddenly realized how important Daniel had become to her, but these kinds of feelings were new to her. She laid down her goose quill. "If only Mother were here," she murmured to herself. "Mother could help me sort all this out."

Then one day late in April Alva went outside, sniffed the mild air, picked up a handful of soil and crumbled it, and returned to announce, "The wet's out of the ground, boys. We'll start plowing tomorrow."

Jessica decided that was about the best thing that could have happened, for now all their days were busy, full of toil that wasn't like winter's indoor work. This was work for backs and shoulders, long hours of it—so much for everybody to do that Daniel's black mood seemed gradually to disappear. Alva taught him how to plow, along with everything else, and Jessica thought it helped. He couldn't keep telling over his grievances to himself, she guessed, when he was taking his turn at plowing, with Buck and Bright straining and pulling in front of him. He had to guide the plow, hold the reins in his teeth, and signal the oxen to turn right or left without the "Gee, gee" and "Haw, haw" that Alva and Linus shouted. Still, he seemed to manage.

Jessica no longer had time to brood, either. The day started for all of them before sunup and went on until long after dark. Spring nights were cool and good for work. Sometimes it would be close to midnight before they came in, ate their late supper, and fell wearily into bed.

While Alva and the boys made the fields ready for

wheat, corn, buckwheat, pumpkins, beans, and potatoes, they also took time to plow a patch near the
cabin for Jessica. This was to be the kitchen garden,
where she'd plant carrots, turnips, beans, beets, cab-
bage, and parsnips, and also herbs like boneset and
tansy, which would be dried and kept for fevers and
aches. Another patch close by would be for her flax.

Jessica had the house in good order and tried to
keep it so, almost as though her mother might walk
in any minute. Likely it was still too early for the
roads to be fit, but she wanted to be prepared. The
new little rocker was in place, and she'd made a
patchwork pillow for it. Secretly she felt sure that the
next letter from Albany would contain the news they
were waiting for.

She went over her supplies, counting and calculating. There were plenty of candles, and there was a
good supply of maple sugar and syrup, for they'd
tapped the maples and sugared off early in April.
Soap was getting low, however, and Jessica decided
to make this herself. It would be one less hard job
for her mother to do when she returned, and what
Jessica made now should be enough to see them
through to November at least. She'd helped with it
many times, so she knew just how it was done. Alva
said he was sure she could manage, but she might
need an extra pair of hands. Daniel would be excused
from work in the fields for one day so that he could
help her with all the lugging and lifting.

Jessica, who was nervous in a happy kind of way
about spending the day with Daniel, made everything
ready for the job and explained it as she went along.
"This barrel here's called a leach barrel. It's got straw

in the bottom to keep the lye from clogging, and we keep adding ashes to it—all the ones we don't take to the ashery to sell. You put in four quarts of lime, too, and then you keep adding water—that's where I throw the dishwater sometimes." They were working in front of the cabin, where a good-sized fire had been built. Daniel nodded, his face serious as he concentrated on what she was saying. "The lye has to be good and strong. If a potato floats in it, it's just right." The barrel sat on a bench by the door, high enough so that the big kettle could be slipped under a wooden spout where the lye could run out. As Jessica explained what had to be done, Daniel filled the kettle and hung it over the fire. Then Jessica went inside and came back with crocks of fat and grease she'd saved—even small bones left over from cooking. They were added to the pot, and she and Daniel took turns stirring. One time he placed his hands over hers as she guided the stick in slow circles, and looked down at her until she pulled her hands away.

"Don't let the lye touch you anywhere," she said, covering her nervousness, "and keep stirring until it gets smooth and those little bones start to disappear."

He looked at her questioningly.

"It's the lye," she explained. "It eats 'em right up. But now it's all turning into soap." Just before they removed it from the fire she threw in some powder. "Ground sassafras bark," she said. "Makes it smell sweet."

When it was done, Daniel looked pleased, as if it was something amazing they'd made together—not just a kettle of soap. He helped her pour it into wooden tubs and they stored it away on the shelf.

That night Jessica wrote in her journal, *I don't want to feel too happy because it might be nothing, but I think Daniel is beginning to return to himself at last.*

There were other spring jobs to be done. Bedding was washed and hung over the fence to dry, after which Jessica's hands were so red and raw she had to rub them with some of Bess's heavy cream. Linus and Daniel drove their small flock of sheep to McGarrity's gristmill to wash them where the water ran over the spillway of the milldam. The warm sun dried them quickly on the way home. Then they were ready for shearing, and Alva did this himself with big shears, cutting off the long fleece skillfully, close to the skin but never nicking an animal.

Planting followed plowing, and by May the apple tree was in bloom outside the cabin door. Jessica was disappointed her mother wasn't there to see it, but Alva assured her she might be with them before all the blossoms dropped. He had an eager look about him these days, she thought.

Then there was green showing in Jessica's kitchen garden and the flax was up. In the barn there were six new lambs and a little heifer that Bess was proud of.

One day Pastor Baldwin came walking out along the river path, smiling and waving something in his hand. Jessica, who was in the dooryard washing fleece in a big tub, was the first to see him, and she put down her wooden paddle and waved back. Alva, working in the near cornfield, came hurrying to the house.

"Knew you'd be too busy to be walking to the village," the minister said. "So I asked for your mail at the store. Two letters from Albany, looks like."

Alva took the letters from him. "And you walked all the way here just to bring them? Why, Pastor, you never should've. Jessie, haven't you some cool buttermilk in the cellar?"

Jessica flew to the cellar, which was really just a hole in the ground back of the cabin, and brought back buttermilk. The minister sat on the doorstep and drank it, and then courtesy demanded that he and Alva chat a little. Jessica was trembling with excitement over the letters, but she managed to stay quiet.

". . . a good-sized force, so they tell," Pastor was saying. "Our men landed near Port Dover, on the far shore of Lake Erie. So it now appears the tide is turning, at least in our part of the state. Now, over toward Lake Champlain's another story, I hear. The British have it in mind to cut off New England from the rest of the union. . . ."

Alva nodded and mumbled something about the Federalists and their shipping interests, all the while fingering the letters he held in his hand. When Pastor Baldwin started to leave, Alva walked with him partway. Jessica could see them talking earnestly and the pastor shaking his head. She guessed that her father was asking if there'd been any word about Daniel's kin.

By the time he got back to the doorstep, the two boys had come in from the fields, sweaty and curious.

"We saw Pastor," Linus said. "Is it mail?"

"It is indeed." Alva sat on the doorstep and they crowded around him as he looked at the two letters.

"Look, Pa," Linus pointed out. "That one isn't in Mother's hand."

"No, you're right, that looks like Grandmother Brock's hand. Well, let's start with Mother's."

He read aloud, " 'Dear husband and children: I can't say just what the delay is in our getting started for home. I have been ready and packed these three weeks, but Mother has put me off, saying the roads are a quagmire. I am so well and strong now, I would buy passage and come by stage, but it costs dearly and I haven't the money.' "

Alva broke off and picked up the other letter. His eyes skimmed over it rapidly. The sun was as warm as summer on their backs as they stood there, but Jessica felt cold creeping into her toes and fingers. Alva got up, walked a few steps away, and then returned. With one hand he rubbed the back of his neck.

"What is it, Pa?" Jessica asked.

"They're not going to let her come back," he said in a tight, pinched voice. "Your grandmother's set on having her stay in Albany."

Chapter

13

"NOT LET HER come back!" Jessica's voice was loud with alarm. "But she belongs with us!"

"Oh, Grandmother allows that she does," Alva said in a dry voice. "What she wants is for us to come there." He read to them from the second letter. " 'If you could see how greatly Ruth has thrived here, I know you would admit the city agrees with her, and that it is the proper place for all of you, where you can enjoy the many comforts and advantages of a more refined society.' "

"Refined society?" Linus, the born farmer, burst out.

"Leave the farm?" Jessica's voice had a hollow, far-away sound to her own ears.

"If it was a man, he could just leave and walk

home," Alva said thoughtfully. "A woman alone couldn't do that."

"There's families coming west all the time," Jessica said. "Couldn't she ride along with someone?"

"Families coming west don't have all that much room to spare, Jessie." Alva glanced down at the letters in his hand. Jessica could picture his mind working over all the possibilities as he tried to think it out in his reasonable way.

"The way I size it up," he said at last, "there's only one thing for me to do. I'll have to go to Albany myself. If Mother's as well as she says and anxious to come back, I'll fetch her."

"You going to walk all that way?" Linus asked.

"It's how I got out here in the first place, son."

"But Mother couldn't walk so far."

"No, she couldn't. To come back I'd need a horse and wagon."

They were all silent, thinking the same thing. There wasn't any money for a horse and wagon. Jessica voiced it hesitantly. "Pa, how could you manage that?"

"That would need some studying out."

"Maybe you could borrow one from somebody," Linus suggested.

Alva shook his head. "Too much to ask. And I'd never be able to return the favor. No, what I'd have to do, I'd have to go to work in Albany for a spell, earn the money. There's work a-plenty on the docks, the boats. I've done it before. You two were just small, but surely you can remember me doing that when we lived in Albany."

They sat quietly for a moment, thinking back.

"I could do it," he went on. "That's not what worries me. It's you young'uns. Leaving you here by yourselves. I might be gone pretty near the whole summer. Could you take care of everything?"

"We could do it, Pa," Linus said at once. "No call to worry about that."

"Of course we could," Jessica said.

"There's haying—you got to do that without fail." Alva got up again and started pacing back and forth, tugging at his beard. "There's hoeing around the corn. The stock to look after. And Jessie, you've got to keep an eye on your flax, not let it get too ripe and toughen up on you."

"We know, Pa. We can do it," Jessica insisted. But to herself she wondered if that could be her voice, speaking out of the hollow place inside her. She knew a moment's hot anger as she thought of Grandmother Brock's neat little carriage, which could so easily carry Ruth Parish home.

Alva studied her. "Don't waste time on hating, Jessie. Hate never plowed the field nor carded the wool. Might's well give it up. Besides, it's your grandma. And likely she's just as sure she's right as you are."

Jessica looked down quickly, ashamed that he could read her so easily, but the anger didn't go away.

"Anyway," Alva said, "you've got an extra pair of hands to help out. You'll do that, won't you, Daniel? Stay and help?"

It was the first time anyone remembered Daniel, they'd all been so preoccupied with the letters. Now, with Alva's hand on his shoulder, Daniel met his eyes squarely and nodded.

They all stood and watched a few days later as Alva

made himself a knapsack, folding a three-foot square of heavy summer cloth cornerwise and then twice more, pinning it at the corners. He put in extra hose and a shirt, a square of Jessica's johnnycake, some dried meat, cornmeal, and salt. He looked to his rifle and ammunition and gave them some last instructions: Trust Mrs. Cosgrove's advice if there was some problem about the farm. If they were in any real need, go to Reverend Mr. Baldwin or Mr. Stillwater. Stillwater's wife might have a sharp tongue, but Moses and Alva had always gotten on well. Moses would look out for them, so they should trust to his counsel. Then without making too many words about it, he said good-bye and started out on the river path headed toward the road that led eastward.

They watched him out of sight. Then the boys turned back to their work in the fields and Jessica went into the cabin to get on with the day's chores. But over and over one thought bounced around in her head.

Now they were really alone.

She had some trouble going to sleep that night. Uneasy thoughts kept plaguing her—thoughts of how far the western New York country was from Albany, of how much responsibility rested on them. Jessica turned restlessly and tried to find a cool place on her pillow. What her mother always said when something was worrisome was, *The best thing to do is study what you can put your hand to. Nothing like useful work to get rid of worry.* Well, there was plenty of work, she told herself sensibly. In a week or so she'd start pulling flax, and maybe Daniel would help her. She closed her eyes, and in her mind she started doing it—pulling the stalks, laying them straight, piling them up. Still pulling, she fell asleep.

They spent the first few days getting used to life around the farm without Alva. Linus and Daniel refigured how to share the chores, and as soon as Jessica's housework was done she went outside to help wherever she was needed. By the end of each day, they were exhausted and a little lonely in the strangely silent cabin. As Jessica prepared to write in her journal one night, she thought with surprise, *Why, tomorrow's my birthday.* The next morning she made a pot of beans and a special batch of cornbread to have with molasses for the birthday dinner. She thought that Linus had forgotten what day it was until he handed her a flat pine board.

"Happy birthday, Jess," he said shyly.

Jessica turned over the board in her hands. It was lap-size, and the corners were rounded and smooth. She looked at Linus.

"Daniel and I worked on it together," he said. "It's for when you write in your journal. We figured you could sit in the new rocking chair and rest the paper on the board in your lap."

Tears came to Jessica's eyes and she wiped at them with the back of her hand. "It's wonderful," she said, and thought that the only thing that could have made her birthday better was if her mother and father had been here with them.

The next morning Jessica and Daniel started on the flax, pulling the whole patch except for the seed plants, which had to ripen fully. They carried the stalks to the little spring-fed stream back of the barn, put them in the water, and weighted them down with rocks.

As they walked back, Jessica pointed out a spot near where the spring rose. "I always thought that little slope right there would be a good place for a springhouse," she said. "I could carry the milk there, and I bet the spring would keep it cool even in hot weather. Better than the cellar behind the house."

Daniel listened and nodded, slowing down to study the spot.

One thing about Daniel, Jessica wrote in her journal that night, her new board sitting comfortably in her lap, *he'll tackle anything. It never bothers him, like it would Linus, that it might be woman's work. He'll churn or gather eggs or help hoe around the vegetables. Once he even tried his hand at the loom, working with my blue and butternut-dyed yarn and showing a good bit of skill, too. Maybe he doesn't mind because he doesn't know the difference. Pa thinks he's never done farm work before, so maybe one job is like another to him.*

After she'd put the idea of the springhouse in his mind, Daniel went to work and drew pictures of it, using charcoal and a smooth board. He showed them to her and Linus, pointing out how he could set it into the bank with timbers to reinforce the ceiling and a door to keep it dark and cold. In the following weeks, whenever Linus could spare him, he went back there to work, digging out and then banging in rocks and stones and finally making a framed entrance and a door with leather hinges. It was high enough so Jessica hardly had to stoop to walk in, and the little room itself was moist and cool, with a shelf and a hard-packed dirt floor. The little spring bubbled at one end and drained out along a narrow ditch lined with stones. Jessica praised it when it was done and declared she'd never seen anything so well made.

One day after milking she carried the bucket back there and strained the milk through a piece of linen. She was about to set the crocks on the shelf to cool when she noticed Daniel standing in the doorway.

"Oh, Daniel," she gasped. "You startled me coming up so quietly like that."

Daniel reached for one of the crocks and put it on the shelf. When he turned to her, his face was serious and he was looking at her in that intense way of his. Jessica felt herself turning red, and for once in her life she couldn't think of anything to say. Daniel leaned toward her and gently brushed her lips with his. She closed her eyes and willed her heart to slow to its normal pace. When she opened her eyes, he was gone. She sat down with a thud, no longer trusting her legs to hold her up, and wondered if she had imagined the whole thing. But the scent of Daniel lingered in the cool darkness, and the strange warm feeling running through her couldn't be something she had dreamed.

Jessica selfishly wished she had nothing to think about except what had happened in the springhouse. But as they sat down to supper that night, Linus said, "I'm worried. Why do you think we don't hear from Pa?"

Something cold wrapped itself around Jessica's

heart. "You think he's had some kind of trouble? He's only been gone four weeks."

"No." Linus's voice was firm. "Not Pa. He's up to handling anything. I'm not worried that way. I'm worried about what he wants us to do."

"We've kept up with everything, just like he said," Jessica pointed out. "We brought in plenty of hay, and the flax is pulled."

Linus nodded. "I know. The corn's ready to be cut now, too, and we can do that all right. It's the wheat I'm worried about. I thought sure we'd hear from Pa before the wheat was ripe."

They were all silent for a moment, thinking about the wheat. It was their biggest crop, and the touchiest, too—they didn't dare let it stand in the field once it ripened, for fear of wet weather getting to it. But could they get it in safely, just the three of them? Alva always said a good farmer took care not to plant more than he could harvest, but he'd figured on being here himself to help, and maybe a couple of other men he'd trade work with. Jessica realized that without saying so out loud they'd all been counting on having him back before the wheat harvest.

"Let's write to him and ask him what he wants us to do," Jessica said. "I can walk into town tomorrow morning and leave the letter at Stillwater's. Who knows," she added with more optimism than she felt, "maybe there will be a letter waiting for us."

"You can't walk to town alone," her brother said firmly. "If Pa were here, he wouldn't let you. And I'm in charge till he gets back."

It seemed to Jessica her brother looked uncommonly pompous when he said things like that. She'd been fifteen since three weeks ago and it didn't sit well with her.

"What a fuss! Mercy, I'd stick right to the river path and be home in no time."

Linus's eyes grew small and beady. "No. You take Daniel with you."

"You just said the corn's ready to be cut," Jessica shot back, purposely not looking in Daniel's direction. "It seems to me that you and Daniel would want to start on that and let me walk to town. I'd be back before you know it."

Linus's jaw remained stubbornly set, but she could see that the corn argument was a powerful one. "I'll think about it" was all he would say.

The next morning, after she promised to stay on the river path and to turn right around and come home if anything didn't look right, Linus let Jessica walk to town. She carried the letter she and Linus had written the night before, and a basket of her best wool, washed and carded and separated into rolls the size of tallow candles. She planned to trade for supplies, and also ask if a letter had come for them. Daniel had seemed withdrawn and brooding this morning. He had headed out to the fields right after breakfast, not even waiting until she set off for town. Just when she thought she understood Daniel, she mused, he'd change and become a different person.

Jessica was so lost in thought that she was surprised to see that the five miles had flown by. Suddenly there was Mr. Gideon Hatch's tannery and then McGarrity's mill, where they'd taken the sheep. The big wheel was turning slowly in the midsummer trickle of the millstream. She paused to watch it for a minute from the cool bank where ferns grew. The first log houses lay just ahead of her, and from a distance she could hear the clang of the black-smith's hammer.

Chapter
14

JESSICA WAS RELIEVED that there was no sign of either Artemas or Mrs. Stillwater when she entered the store. She walked over and placed her basket of wool on the counter.

"Morning, Mr. Stillwater."

Moses Stillwater looked up from his account book and smiled at her. "Well, Jessie! I've been wondering when we'd see you. Everything all right out there at your place?"

"Yes indeed, thank you. We're managing just fine. I have a letter to send to Albany." She paused. "I don't suppose there's a letter from my father. . . ."

Moses's voice held genuine regret. "I surely would like to say yes, but there ain't, Jessie. I wouldn't place any meaning on it, though. Mail from the east gets delayed more often than not. Ever since the fighting out west, transport for the troops comes first. Mail gets sent whenever they have a free stagecoach." He shook his head at the arrangement.

"Yes, I daresay that's it." Jessica hadn't realized how disappointed she'd be. "Well, then," she said brightly, "I'll give you our letter, and perhaps you'd like to look at this wool. Our sheep did real well this year, and I brought you the very longest staple. We need salt and molasses."

"Say, that does look mighty fine," he said, leaning over the counter and fingering the wool. Then in a low voice he added, "What about the boy? You decide what to do with him?"

"I don't know as we'll decide anything till Mother and Father get home," she said.

"But you're not frightened, you and your brother? You think he's all *right?*" Moses's face had a worried look that Jessica couldn't help thinking was funny. Almost everyone seemed to believe that because Daniel couldn't speak he must not be right in the head.

"Oh, he's been mighty helpful to us," she said.

"That so?" Moses marveled. Jessica was relieved he made no mention of Artemas. He turned to measure out the salt and molasses, and Jessica's gaze wandered to the window. She stifled a gasp as she saw Daniel standing just outside. He was looking beyond her and over her head to a shelf behind the counter where Moses kept some of the choicer items he'd taken in trade. Westward-bound pioneers often found, by the time they got this far, that salt and flour were a good deal more important than cherished possessions they'd brought with them. So they'd leave behind the things on the shelf—a book with a title in gold on its spine, *Modern Medicinal Remedies;* a china teapot with pink roses; a straight razor with an ivory handle. Next to the razor was the prettiest little inkwell she'd ever seen, small and round and made of cut glass with a hinged silver top and a silver tray to rest on. It looked as dainty and fine as a lady's teacup.

There were two thumps as Moses hoisted the bag of salt and jug of molasses to the counter. Jessica glanced quickly toward the window, but Daniel was gone.

"There we are," he said cheerfully. "And a length of ribbon for you, young lady." Moses always gave something to boot.

"Oh, I do thank you," she said politely, then hurried out of the store as fast as she could without being rude. She didn't see Daniel anywhere. Jessica remembered Linus's warning to come directly home, but she decided she would spend just a few minutes looking for Daniel. As she rounded the back of the store someone grabbed her arm, and her basket went flying.

"Artemas! You scared me to death," she said, whirling toward him. He was sweaty and slightly mussed, as if he had been working at something—which Jessica was sure was not the case.

"What are you doing back here?" he hissed.

"I . . . Oh, I . . ." She struggled to free herself from his grasp, but he held her tightly.

"You're looking for the dummy, aren't you?" His face was close to hers, and she could see the beads of sweat on his upper lip. "I saw him watching you through the window. He ran off when he saw me.

Guess I scared him. He's probably some kind of army deserter, a coward like that."

"Artemas, you let go of me this instant!" Jessica said firmly. Instead, he pulled her closer. Jessica kicked out with her foot at the same time that she pulled and twisted with all her might. Artemas winced in pain and grabbed his shin, and Jessica went sprawling backward into the dirt. Suddenly Daniel was standing between her and Artemas. She got up hurriedly, brushing dust from herself, and grabbed her basket.

"Come on, Daniel," she said, taking his arm.

But Daniel stood still, his face white with hatred, his eyes boring into Artemas, who had shrunk back against the building. Daniel clutched something tightly in his left fist, and Jessica worried it was a stone meant for Artemas's head. Artemas cowered against the wall of the store, still rubbing his shin.

"Daniel, please!" she cried.

Slowly he turned toward her and let the stone fall from his hand. He didn't resist as she pulled him toward home.

They walked single file in silence. Daniel, carrying Jessica's basket with the salt and molasses, kept his eyes to the ground. Jessica hated to see him turn inward like this again, and she guessed he might be thinking about his life before he came to them. She had been scared at the look on his face back at the store, and she had to admit there was an awful lot they didn't know about Daniel.

Linus was waiting for them at the house, and Jessica could tell by the worried look on his face that he was to blame for Daniel's following her. She couldn't be mad at him, but she would have to wait until Daniel was out of earshot to relate the day's events. Instead she said, "There was no letter from Pa, but I left ours with Mr. Stillwater. He said the mail's been slow from the east." She glanced to the loft, where Daniel had gone as soon as they got home, and then busied herself with the noon meal.

In the afternoon heat they all worked at the corn, slashing and cutting with their sharp corn knives until long after dark, since the moon was full. When they finally ate their late supper of johnnycake and milk and fell into their beds, it seemed to Jessica she could sleep till victory and salvation, as her father always said.

But she didn't. The scream that woke her was so piercing and fearful that it cut through sleep the way Alva's sharp skinning knife cut through a hide. Jessica sat up in bed, her heart thumping, frozen with fear for a minute. Then she jumped out of bed and ran barefooted into the cabin's main room, over to the foot of the loft ladder. She could hear a commotion overhead, and Linus's voice, sleepy but anxious, saying something she couldn't make out. She grabbed the ladder and climbed up. She had an impression of arms flailing around in the dark.

"There now. Whoa. Hold up, Daniel."

Linus was talking the way he did to Bess when she acted ornery and whipped her tail at him. He seemed to have left his own pallet to struggle with Daniel. There was no more screaming, just panting and thrashing sounds. Gradually they stopped.

"Jess?" Linus crept over to where she was hanging on to the top of the ladder.

"What happened?" she whispered.

"Nightmare, I reckon. He's all right now." Jessica couldn't see his smile but she could hear it as he added, "He's got a voice right enough, hasn't he?"

They all slept past sunup, and Daniel was the last one up. Linus had to call him twice, and when he came down the ladder he still looked sleepy.

Linus said, "We did so well with that corn yesterday, likely Daniel and I can finish it up without you today, Jess."

Jessica was relieved. She'd let the chores around the house slide these last few days. This would give her a chance to tidy things up, and then perhaps she'd have time to work at her flax in the front dooryard.

Later, after the two boys left for the fields and she was sweeping around the hearth, she happened to glance up toward the spot where Alva had stuck Daniel's knife in the log last Christmas.

The knife was gone.

Chapter
15

JESSICA WAS ALONE in the dooryard late in the morning when Moses Stillwater drove up in his wagon. Linus and Daniel were still working on the corn, almost out of sight in the east field. Jessica was breaking flax, the part that had rotted earliest back in the stream. She'd let the sun dry it thoroughly and now she was pounding it, a handful at a time, with the big hinged beam of the flax brake. As Jessica raised the beam and whacked it down, the dust and straw went flying, lodging in her hair and clinging to her dress. But once the outer part of the plant fell away, there in the center was the beautiful pale gray fiber. Crackling flax was certainly one of the meanest jobs there was, Jessica admitted, but like most hard jobs, it had its reward.

She was sure, the minute she saw Mr. Stillwater's

wagon, that a letter had come from Albany, and her heart gave a great leap of excitement that made her feel for a minute almost light-headed.

"Morning, Mr. Stillwater," she called out to him when he was still barely within hailing distance. She put down the brake beam and brushed at her hair and the front of her dress. "Real warm morning to drive out from town." She wanted him to know she appreciated his making the special trip. But oddly, he made no reply—didn't even lift his hand in greeting. He stopped the horse and climbed down slowly and heavily. Jessica could see there wasn't any letter in his hand. Fear knotted up inside her.

"Is something wrong? You've had word of Father?"

He shook his head. "Your brother at home, Jessie?"

"He's yonder cutting corn." She nodded toward the field. "I can go fetch him—"

"Oh well, it's no matter. I can tell you."

"Let me draw you a cool drink."

He shook his head and put up a hand to stop her. "No. I felt I had to ride out and tell you. You two young'uns are here by yourselves and I knew it'd be on my mind."

"Tell us what? What is it?" Something in the back of her mind said, *Daniel.*

Moses mopped his forehead with his handkerchief. "There was an inkwell I took in trade a while back. Had a real silver tray to it. The thing is, it's gone. And Artemas told me he saw Daniel hanging around the store yesterday, looking in the window."

Jessica felt herself redden. She tried to say something, but no words came. Moses Stillwater seemed to recognize her embarrassment. "No need to say anything," he said. His hand came up, then dropped. "I ain't blaming you and Linus any. Only I know right well that boy took it. All right, it's gone. It's no matter, anyway, alongside the other worries I got. That's the reason I drove out here. Now I know you folks have taken a fancy to him and all, but I don't care what you say. He's not right in the head. If he was, he'd be able to tell us where he comes from and who his people are. And a boy who'd steal, well, he might do other mischief, too. Or worse than mischief. I sure would hate to hear of something happening to you and Linus. You're out here all alone, no near neighbor to hear you—"

He broke off with a helpless gesture. Jessica stood there speechless, almost unable to draw breath. Her hands were like two cold stones.

"Oh, Mr. Stillwater," she said at last, "I just can't believe—" But then she stopped. What did she believe, anyway? The thought of that missing knife had been hammering through her head all morning with every whack of the flax brake. She cursed that big fat Artemas for stirring up trouble again. Most likely Daniel had been in town only to check up on her. She had half a mind to tell Mr. Stillwater that Artemas had grabbed her behind the store.

"I'd best be getting back," Moses said. "But I just wouldn't have rested easy if I hadn't told you. You and your brother talk it over. Let me know if you want help. I could send somebody out for him, see that he's shut up someplace till we study out what to do with him." He walked with slow steps back to his wagon and climbed in. "Now that I've told you, I don't know as I'll rest easy anyway."

She said nothing to Linus about it until late afternoon, when Daniel went out to the barn to milk. Linus, coming in from the cornfield, stopped outside the door to splash his hot face in the bucket of water that stood on the bench there. He was rubbing it dry with an old piece of tow cloth when Jessica came to the door and told him to step inside for a minute.

"What for?"

"Never mind," she said, pulling his arm, "just come in."

He stepped into the cabin, and while Jessica went about preparing supper—taking a pot of stew from the fireplace, bringing a fresh loaf of bread from the shelf—she told him everything that had happened in town yesterday and about Moses's visit and what he'd said. Then, more hesitantly, she told him about the missing knife. Linus's eyes went up to the empty gash in the wall.

He said nothing except "Where?" and "When?" as she talked, and after she'd finished he stood silent for a long time. Then at last he said, "There's only one thing to it. Do we trust him still or don't we?"

"I trust him," Jessica said stoutly.

Linus was silent for a moment. "But do you think he stole it?"

"If you trust someone—" Jessica was having a hard time keeping her voice from quavering. "If you trust someone, you don't give up on him the first time something goes against him or makes him look in the wrong. I don't think he stole it, but if he did, he must have had a reason."

"Still, it sounds awful bad."

"Linus, I can't help it. I believe in Daniel. I just do, that's all."

There was a long silence in the cabin. Late afternoon sunlight poured in from the west, throwing Linus's shadow clear across the puncheon floor from doorway to fireplace. At last he said, "Well, so do I. But I'm going to have to ask him about it. And he'll have to give me the knife."

"Yes," she agreed soberly. "He'll have to do that."

For a time they stood thinking their separate thoughts, and only when they moved again did they realize that another shadow lay across the floor beside Linus's. Daniel was standing in the doorway. She hoped he hadn't overheard their talk.

At suppertime he ate poorly. Jessica heaped his plate and spread butter on a slab of bread for him, but he only poked at his food.

"I declare, you don't look well, Daniel," she said.

"Too much sun, more'n likely," Linus agreed.

"You'd better turn in early," Jessica said. "Linus and I'll finish up the chores."

After supper he surprised them by climbing the ladder to the loft almost at once. There were sounds of moving about and then he was quiet. Likely he was worn out, Jessica thought. But if he was wakeful later, she'd brew him up some mayflower tea.

Linus went to the barn to finish the chores. Jessica washed the dishes and tidied the hearth, then walked out to the springhouse to see if Daniel had strained the milk. But of course he had, and even that made her sad, the way he never neglected his work, even when he was feeling poorly. There stood the jugs on the shelf, the milk all strained and set for the cream to rise. She let herself think just for a minute of that other time in the springhouse. Everything was different now. Daniel was different. She closed the heavy door behind her and turned back toward the house. Westward, past the river, the sunset was turning the whole sky to red and orange. She watched the light deepen the gold of the wheat that stretched out almost as far as she could see. It caught on the shingle roof of the cabin and struck rosy lights there. The whole farm looked rich and full of promise, just as it should with harvest time approaching. If only her parents would get here—they'd know what to do to help Daniel.

In the tall grass before her something moved, and Jessica smiled as she watched. There was a small meow as Floss's last kitten, the one Jessica called Boots, came into view, leggy and half grown now. This one had been the puniest, but as sometimes happened, it turned out smart and wily, and it followed anyone walking toward the springhouse, knowing that was where the milk was carried. Jessica shook her head, but she opened the door again and brought out a saucer of milk for the kitten. Then she sat in the grass and watched as the pink tongue flashed in and out, the whiskers twitching with pleasure.

The western sky faded from orange to rose to lavender, and then the lavender became blue-gray. When she heard Linus calling her, she got up and started back toward the cabin. The kitten followed her.

Linus had lighted a candle indoors and he stood in the doorway against its faint light. Jessica had an uneasy feeling.

"What is it?"

"Come here," he said. "Look." He motioned her inside and she saw that he was holding something—the little cut-glass inkwell sitting in its silver tray. Jessica gave a gasp and put her hand to her mouth. "I found it on the table just now when I came in," Linus said.

Jessica's glance flew to the loft ladder.

"He's gone," Linus said.

She felt a stinging against her eyelids. "Oh, Linus, no! I knew he didn't look right tonight."

"That's not all. Look here." He motioned her over to the table. Beside the candle was a piece of paper. Jessica read it.

I am sorry for causing you so much trouble.

Chapter 16

J ESSICA LOOKED AT her brother. "Linus!"

"I know. He can write."

"But he doesn't write like us."

"No, he doesn't, for a fact." They both looked again at the scrap of paper. It wasn't the kind of hand they'd learned in the village school from Pastor Baldwin's wife. It was a fine, slender hand with all the letters slanting one way. Each word started with a smooth little curl.

Linus put down the inkwell and walked over to the open door. "I don't know where to start looking, but there's still a good moon tonight."

"You don't think he went after Artemas, do you? After what happened in town yesterday . . ." Jessica looked worriedly at her brother.

"I don't know, but I'll head toward town first. If

there's no sign of him that way then I'll double back toward the Cosgroves' place."

Jessica was taking her shawl down from its peg and hurrying to join him.

"Where do you think you're going?" Linus demanded.

"With you. And don't you dare act bossy and try to stop me, for I won't be stopped."

Linus looked at her and seemed to decide that he'd best not argue with her.

They searched and scoured every inch of the way along the river path to the village, calling Daniel's name. A dozen times Jessica went over to the bank and peered down. "Linus, he could have missed his footing and fallen right in."

"Come on! Keep looking," Linus said, his face cross and worried.

Jessica and Linus walked through the village, already still and sleeping except for one or two lights. There had been no sign of Daniel along the way. As they neared Stillwater's store Linus motioned for Jessica to stop and be still. "I thought I heard something," he whispered, but everything was empty and quiet. Jessica shivered in spite of the warm night.

"What now?" she whispered to Linus.

"I'm going up a little farther. You stay here in case he comes to the store. I'll be back in a minute." Linus disappeared into the darkness.

Jessica flattened herself against the back wall of Stillwater's store, feeling less brave now that she was alone. The silence of the sleeping town surrounded her. Once she thought she heard a scuffling sound, but when she peeked around the corner of the store the street was empty.

She tried to think about places Daniel might have gone. They'd searched the town and couldn't find him. What if he'd gone in another direction? Jessica inched toward the front of the store. The town, so familiar and comforting by day, now seemed a strange, almost scary place. She looked in all directions and was just about to go back and wait for Linus when a movement caught her eye. She fixed the spot in her mind and, staying out of the moonlight, crept forward as fast as she dared. She started to call Daniel's name, but something told her to be still.

She had almost reached McGarrity's mill when she heard a loud thud. It seemed to come from behind the mill, where the ground dropped sharply to the river. She moved toward the sound, trying to walk quietly on the uneven ground. As she reached the rear of the mill her hand flew to her mouth to stifle a gasp, for not twenty feet in front of her stood Artemas. And Daniel was lying at his feet.

Jessica ducked behind some large logs that were waiting to be milled and watched in horror as Artemas gave Daniel a shove with his foot and sent him rolling down the bank toward the river. There was the sound of a splash, and Artemas gave a satisfied grunt and turned to leave. Jessica held her breath as Artemas walked by close enough that she could touch him. As soon as he rounded the front of the mill, she half ran, half slid down the bank.

"Daniel," she called in a loud whisper. "Daniel, where are you?" She ran along the river, first one way and then the other, looking for him, the reflection of the moon on the water giving her only a little help. Tears of frustration made it still harder to see. She scrabbled downstream, clawing at clods of dirt and small shrubs to keep from tumbling into the river. She came upon him so suddenly she almost tripped over him, lying as he was half in and half out of the slow-moving water.

"Daniel, can you hear me?" she whispered frantically as she bent over him. "Daniel, it's me, Jessica."

He gave no sign that he heard her, not the turn of his head nor the blinking of his eyes. She grabbed his arm and pulled as hard as she could, then splashed into the water to lift his legs onto dry land. She dug at the damp ground with her hands, furiously pushing her hair from her sweating face, to make a spot where he wouldn't roll back toward the water. When she was sure he was secure she stood up.

"Don't move, Daniel," she commanded, not knowing if he could hear her or not, and went to look for Linus.

She found him not far from the mill. The worried look on his face only grew more worried when he saw her.

"Where have you been and what happened to you?" he asked gruffly, eyeing her wet clothes, dirty face, and flyaway hair.

"I've found Daniel but he's hurt bad, Linus," she said breathlessly. "Hurry! He's down by the river."

Together they made their way down the bank. Linus bent over the figure. "Oh, Jess." His face was white in the moonlight as he looked up at her.

She sank down next to her brother. She wasn't sure

she could speak, her mouth was that dry. "Is he . . . ,"
she croaked.

"He's alive. But we've got to get him tended to. He's
bleeding pretty bad. Give me your shawl." Jessica un-
tied the shawl hurriedly and Linus secured it around
Daniel's right shoulder, where most of the blood
seemed to be coming from. As he worked he told Jessica, "We'll take him to Widow Cosgrove. It'll be closer
than taking him home. And she's got herbs and medi-
cines and will know what to do."

She heard Linus panting and struggling, then saw
him in dim outline as he staggered to his feet. Daniel's limp body hung over his shoulders. Daniel
groaned as Linus picked him up. "Sorry Daniel,"
Linus said softly, "but we've got to get you some
help."

Linus walked downstream until he found a section
of the bank that wasn't as steep and where animals
had worn a small path. Jessica trailed after him feeling utterly useless, yet grateful that Linus had taken
control. She felt a sudden weariness that reached all
the way into her bones.

She slowed her footsteps, took a deep breath, and
tried to concentrate on what she had seen behind the
mill. Why would Artemas attack Daniel? Had Daniel
started a fight? Jessica knew he was furious at the
way Artemas had acted yesterday, but she couldn't
believe that Daniel—either one of them, for that matter—would start a fight over it. The little glass inkwell was part of it, of course. He'd taken it, no
question about that. Yet he'd left it behind when he
fled. And she still wouldn't use the word *stolen* when
she thought of it. Daniel wasn't the kind to steal.

Sometimes you knew something about a person without being able to explain how you knew it.

Why had Daniel gone into town without telling them? All this time she'd been so sure he felt safe with them, that he trusted them. There was still that far-off look that came into his eyes sometimes, but she'd never imagined that he would run off and do something foolish—even dangerous. Her eyes grew misty with tears. She brushed at them and kept walking. Try as she might, she couldn't make everything fit together. And nothing would be gained by dwelling on it now. The important thing was to get Daniel tended to.

Widow Cosgrove came to the door in her nightdress, an old quilt thrown around her.

"He's been hurt," Linus said. "We found him in town."

She looked anxiously at Daniel. "He's taken a good beating. And this could be a knife wound," she said, looking at his shoulder. She felt his forehead. "He's feverish. Set him down, Linus, here in front of the hearth." She motioned them inside. "Don't look life-threatening, but we've got to get that wound tended to and get a proper bandage on it."

Following the widow's orders, Linus bathed Daniel's head with a cool cloth while Jessica brewed a tea of adder's-tongue and self-heal. Asa and Leander, who had been wakened by the excitement, were sent to the scrap pile for pieces of cloth to use for a bandage. When the tea was ready, Jessica cradled Daniel's head in her lap and gently spoon-fed him the mixture.

Widow Cosgrove put the last strip of cloth bandage in place. She stood and circled around Daniel, looking at the still figure from every angle. She bent over him, sniffed, put a hand on him, and stood back and looked again. He tossed restlessly.

"Fever, all right," she admitted. "But maybe it ain't mortal. Linus, you take over feeding him that medicine. Jessie, you're a sight. You get cleaned up and then stretch out somewheres and sleep a little. It'll be a while before the medicine takes a hold, no sense all of us standin' around starin' at him. And I'm not lettin' you children walk home alone in the dark."

Now that Daniel had help, Jessica gave in to the weariness. She got most of the mud off her hands and face and made no protest as the widow led her to a quilt in the corner of the room. As she sank down she turned and gave a last look to where the widow was bent over Daniel, talking to Linus.

"I set great store by self-heal," Jessica heard her saying. "And you can't beat adder's-tongue. Grows right there in those woods where it's damp and mossy. I dry it and then grind it." Her pigtail hung untidily down her back. The hem was, as usual, out of her nightdress in the back so that it hung in a draggle. Crouching over Daniel, she looked like a small busy witch. Jessica didn't know as she'd ever been so glad of anybody's help in her whole life. She pulled the quilt around her and felt sleep folding over her like a big soft wing.

Chapter 17

IT WAS PAST noon when Jessica and Linus set out for home. He insisted there was no need for her to come, but she wanted to, and the widow offered to let Daniel stay with her until he was well enough to walk home.

"He's pickin' up some already," she said cheerfully. "Sleepin' sound, and his breath don't rattle so. I'll keep a watch. You've fed him up so good, filled him out, he'll get over this in no time, I'll wager." Her brow creased momentarily in a troubled look. "I'd just like to get my hands on whoever done this to him," she said, shaking her head.

On the way home, Jessica debated how much to tell Linus of what had happened, but in the end she decided this was no time to be keeping secrets. Ma and Pa were still gone and Daniel was in trouble—Linus had to know everything.

He was as puzzled as she was about Daniel's running off and tangling with Artemas. "It doesn't make sense for either one of them to be so riled up and let things go this far," he said. Anxious and apprehensive, they passed their thoughts back and forth as they walked along in the late summer sunshine.

When they got home, Jessica washed herself, combed her hair, and put on a clean linsey shortgown. Linus said the words she had been thinking but couldn't bring herself to say.

"We've got to return the inkwell, Jess. Whatever else happened, Daniel took it. Let's return the pesky thing and be done with it."

They walked the five miles into town in silence, Jessica holding the inkwell and its silver tray tight in both hands. Today she was not as lucky as last time, for all the Stillwaters were present at the store. Moses was behind the counter, deep in conversation with a man Jessica didn't recognize. A traveler or hunter by the look of him, she thought, for he wore buckskins rather than linsey or tow, even though it was summer. Mrs. Stillwater was rearranging bolts of calico on the shelf and Artemas was lounging near her, cleaning his fingernails with the tip of a knife. When he saw Jessica, he slipped the knife into his pocket, smiled, and smoothed his shirtfront where a dribble of grease had made a spot. Jessica tried to keep her face neutral, but more than anything she wanted to get another look at that knife. It surely looked a lot like Daniel's.

"Morning, Jessica, Linus," Artemas said.

"Morning, Artemas, Mrs. Stillwater." Jessica saw the storekeeper's wife glare angrily at the inkwell in her hands, but at that moment Moses looked up and saw them.

"Well, I declare!" he exclaimed.

"We're returning your property, Mr. Stillwater," Jessica said, putting the inkwell down on the counter. "We're mighty sorry you were put out any. I'm sure Daniel meant no harm." She saw Mr. Stillwater's eyes flicker toward Artemas.

"Well now, you didn't have to walk all the way in here just to do that," he said. "I shouldn't have stewed so about it, but I was concerned for you two is all."

"We do thank you for that," Jessica said politely. Suddenly she heard herself say, "Daniel's gone, anyway." She squeezed Linus's hand, warning him to be quiet. "He left us a note last night saying he was sorry for causing so much trouble. He left the inkwell sitting on the note."

Mr. Stillwater was watching her closely.

"Maybe it's just as well," she went on. "We didn't know much about him." She held her breath, afraid Linus might give her away or that Mr. Stillwater might not believe her. She had never been good at fibbing.

But Moses said, "Well, I'm sorry to hear that. But just put all that to one side." There was excitement in his voice. "Important things to talk about today. I've got word for you—from your pa."

"A letter?" Jessica's heart gave a leap.

"Nope, not a letter. Better'n a letter. This fellow here's just rode west from Albany on a fast horse. Talked to your pa not a week ago."

Linus and Jessica turned at once and looked into the stranger's bright blue eyes.

112

"Make you acquainted with Amos Vanderpool," Moses said. "He's headin' towards Pennsylvania. Come into my store inquirin' for the Parish place."

They greeted the man politely in spite of their impatience, and Linus asked, "What message did our father send, Mr. Vanderpool?"

"Is he starting back soon?" Jessica burst out.

"Well, no, little lady, he ain't," Amos Vanderpool replied. "And if I got the straight of it, he ain't comin' back a-tall." His thin, sun-browned face fell into troubled creases, as if he was trying to remember it all correctly.

"Not coming home?" Jessica's eyes widened.

"We thought sure by harvest time—" Linus added.

"Yes, to be sure, he mentioned the harvest. Hold on a minute till I put all the words in order." The creases around his eyes deepened as Linus and Jessica fidgeted. "Now here's the way he spoke. He says your ma's considerable improved livin' there in Albany, and he's got himself work on the docks. He thinks the best thing would be for you young'uns to come back there to live." Amos Vanderpool, obviously a man who made his bed under the stars every night, shook his head slightly at the madness of anyone's preferring city life. Then he continued, "He says what he wants you to do is sell the farm, and once you do that you can buy a hoss and wagon to make the trip."

"Sell the farm?" Linus echoed.

Warning bells went off in Jessica's head. Something was dreadfully wrong here; she just couldn't put it all together yet. She glanced at her brother. Linus's face had paled under his freckles.

"What about the harvest?" Linus asked. "We've got wheat ready to cut."

"What he said was, leave the harvest. Tell 'em not to linger, he said. Just hustle and come on back east." The bright blue eyes looked from one to the other. "He seemed in a powerful hurry. Anxious, like."

Moses Stillwater regarded them soberly. Off to one side, and out of earshot, Mrs. Stillwater inched closer. "Well, now," Moses said, "that's a big dose of news for you young'uns." His plump face sagged into worry.

Something is wrong! The words screamed through Jessica's head. Mrs. Stillwater was edging closer, handkerchief at the ready.

Moses put a comforting arm around each of them. "We got to think this through, that's the nub of it. If it's what your pa wants and the farm's got to be sold, I'll help somehow." He was frowning, as if unsure how he was going to manage this. "I'll ride out to your place in a day or so and we'll try to find some way to work things out."

"But you can't sell a farm all in a minute," Linus said. "Even a good farm, it takes time—"

"Mr. Stillwater's right, Linus," Jessica interrupted, taking her brother's arm and leading him toward the door. "We'll figure some way out. Let's go home and think things over."

Moses walked them to the door.

"Thank you very kindly, Mr. Stillwater," Jessica said, and Linus turned to thank Amos Vanderpool, too. Jessica could feel Artemas's eyes following them out.

They said nothing for a time as they started toward home on the river path. Once Jessica glanced at her brother, marching along in tight-lipped silence, his sunstruck hair a fiery halo around his head. She saw his broad shoulders, the rough hands clenched at his sides.

Then at last they came in sight of their own farm and saw the broad fields of wheat flung out to the horizon. Jessica realized they had been so preoccupied with Amos Vanderpool's message that they had walked right by the turnoff to the Cosgroves' farm without giving a thought to Daniel. They both stopped in the path and looked at their place, taking in the ripe expanse of it. Jessica peeked at Linus. A muscle in his cheek was working away, twitching as if his jaws were clenching and unclenching.

"Linus, did you believe Amos Vanderpool?" she asked.

"Why would he lie? I mean, Pa must have reasons we don't know about," Linus said.

"There was something that didn't sound right to me," Jessica said.

"Didn't any of it sound right to me," Linus said bleakly. "But we'll have to do it—it's what Pa wants."

"But he said to leave the harvest."

"Yes, he did say that."

"But that doesn't sound like Pa!" Jessica burst out. "Can you hear him saying that, Linus?"

He shook his head slowly. "No. I can't." Linus kicked furiously at a stone in the pathway. "If I could just talk to him myself!"

"Think about it, Linus," Jessica said. "No word from Pa in all these months, not a single letter, even though we wrote to him asking him what to do. Then all of a sudden Amos Vanderpool shows up and tells us to sell the farm." Jessica paused. She was thinking out loud now more than talking to Linus. "And Daniel . . . what happened to Daniel is all connected somehow. If only we could figure out how."

Linus muttered something about chores he had to do and headed for the barn. Jessica walked toward the springhouse. Only yesterday she'd watched the sun go down, thinking how proud she was of all they'd accomplished this summer. Thinking how she longed for her parents to see it. Her hand moved up to touch the door of the springhouse. That moment out here with Daniel seemed half a world away now.

Floss's kitten Boots joined her, as he always did when she went to the springhouse. She picked him up, stroking his fur. "We've never disobeyed Pa," she told the kitten. "Not in any big way. But we're going to disobey him twice now. We're *not* going to sell the farm, and we're *not* going to trust Moses Stillwater."

Chapter 18

WHEN JESSICA WOKE up the next morning she had to lie still to think what it was that weighed upon her. She reached for her journal and reread what she had written last night. *Word has come from Pa that we are to sell the farm and move back east to Albany. I know he said to trust to Moses Stillwater's counsel, but something doesn't sit right with me about the whole business.* She sighed and pulled herself out of bed and got dressed. She wouldn't accomplish anything lying in bed all morning. Linus seemed to be already up and outside somewhere. She blew on the coals and built up the fire, mixed the johnnycake and put it in the pan—doing all the morning chores from habit, but her mind was a jumble of thoughts. Could Amos Vanderpool have been telling the truth? What did Moses Stillwater know about the fight between

Daniel and Artemas? Had she seen Artemas slip Daniel's knife into his pocket? How could they get in touch with their pa to get this sorted out, and why hadn't he answered their letters? While the johnnycake was baking in the dutch oven, she swept with her willow broom and then polished the panes of the new window.

Shortly after breakfast Widow Cosgrove came by and reported that Daniel had slept comfortably all night. "Give him one more good night's rest and some more of the medicine, I wouldn't doubt he might even get his legs under him tomorrow. That wasn't a stab wound in his shoulder, near as I can guess. Just a bad cut from when he fell down the bank." She paused, studying Jessica's face. "What's amiss? Did you figure out what happened to him?"

"We think he must have lost his footing in the dark and rolled down the bank," Jessica said, looking at her feet. She hated fibbing to the widow, but after all she'd done for them, it seemed unfair to involve her in any more of their problems. "But that sure is good news you've brought us."

"I'm not worried about Daniel any longer," the widow said. "You're the one's got me concerned. What's troubling you, child?"

"Oh, Mrs. Cosgrove," Jessica said, trying to hold back tears. "Mr. Stillwater told us he had word from Pa. Says we're to sell the farm and come to Albany to live." She brushed away the tears that stubbornly spilled from her eyes. "I don't believe it for a minute, but I'm so mixed up. If only I could talk to Pa."

"There now," the widow said, putting comforting arms around Jessica. "There's got to be a way to figure this out. Don't do nothin' right away. Think on it a spell and the right decision will come to you."

After the widow left, Jessica swept the hearth and let the fire die down. She'd cook outside today, she decided. She went over to her loom and worked a row or two, but presently she just sat there with the wooden shuttle in her hand, feeling the silence of waiting. Moses Stillwater had said he'd come today or tomorrow. Jessica and Linus had to sort things out and decide what to do by then. She listened nervously for the sound of distant wheels, but the day passed quietly with no sign of Moses.

Late in the afternoon, Linus said, "Do you think we should go to Widow Cosgrove's to check on Daniel?"

Jessica wanted to go more than anything, but dreaded having to lie to their neighbor again. "Mrs. Cosgrove was here this morning and said he's mending well. He'll probably get better quicker if we don't disturb him," she told Linus.

They spent the rest of the day without talking, taking comfort in each other's company but lost in their own thoughts.

The next day, shortly after breakfast, Jessica heard a carriage approaching. Linus must have been watching from the barn, for he came in and announced, "It's him." And then, "Oh, damn. He's brought Artemas with him."

Linus wasn't allowed to swear, but Jessica didn't remind him of it this morning.

"Well, now," Moses said after a large swallow of cool cider, "I been studying on this business of the farm and I'm still sorry over it. It ain't often you get as good a man as your pa settling out here. He and

I have been friends since he first came here and built this cabin. I sure hate to lose him—the rest of you, too. But if I take his meaning aright, he's anxious for you to go back there to Albany. So whatever his reasons are, they must be good ones, and we'll have to go along with 'em."

They were sitting at the table, Moses leaning forward heavily on his elbows, Artemas in a careless pose with one arm flung over the back of the chair. Artemas had already drained his mug of cider in one gulp, and perversely, Jessica didn't offer him more.

"But hang it all, it ain't that easy to sell a farm, just as you said yourself the other day, Linus," Moses went on. "Takes talk and bargaining, and you got to find someone with money in his pocket. But here's the way I see it. I know your pa's counting on me to help you out, and I want to, too. So the best I can figger to do is, I'll buy the farm myself. Give you a fair price, you can count on that. Then you can clear out and head east soon as you're of a mind to."

Clear out . . . head east . . . I'll buy the farm myself. The words rattled in Jessica's head.

"*You'd* buy it?" Linus sounded surprised. "Sell it later on to someone else, you mean?"

"Well, that would be one way to do it," Moses said. "I'm a businessman, and it would make good sense. But there was another idea I had. We talked it over some last night."

Something nagged in the back of Jessica's mind. She knew that if she could grasp the thought, she would be closer to understanding the mystery of the last few days.

"What I might do is keep it," Moses said.

"Go into farming yourself?" Linus sounded amazed.

"Well, no. 'Twouldn't be for me. 'Twould be for Artemas."

As though at a signal, Linus and Jessica both looked at Artemas, still sitting in that easy pose with one arm hooked back. He looked different today, Jessica thought. Not slow and lazy and petulant, but thoughtful and planning. As if something was working right now behind those light, narrowed eyes.

Moses seemed to read their surprise. "Artemas needs to pick a profession pretty soon," he said. "He doesn't fancy storekeeping, but it might be he'd want to take up the law or politics—maybe even stand for the legislature. Something like that. And if he does, why, he ought to have property, some kind of land holdings. That's why I thought maybe this place— and it would help you folks out, too."

Help us, or help the Stillwaters to our farm? Jessica asked silently.

"Only thing is," Linus said, and Jessica could tell he was struggling to stay courteous and reasonable, "a farm has to be worked at—kept up—or 'tisn't worth a shilling. And I don't know as Artemas has the—" He paused awkwardly. "—the experience."

Jessica guessed how he must feel at the idea of Artemas walking *his* fields, tending *his* stock. Thinking about what she had seen behind McGarrity's mill, she felt her anger rising and prayed she'd be able to keep silent and not let on what she knew.

"Oh, I daresay he could manage if he had some experienced help to get him started," Moses said, although Jessica could hear the uncertainty in his voice. "Only now, like it or not, we've got to talk price,

121

for I want to be fair about it. If you'll take me around your boundaries, Linus, and show me your stock, why then maybe we can agree on what the place is worth."

"There was more," Artemas said suddenly as his father made to get up from the table. It was the first time he'd entered the conversation, and Jessica was startled. The words were so direct, so confident.

Moses hesitated, glancing toward his son. "Well, yes. There was." He sank back onto the chair. "I don't know as it's the right time to bring it up, I don't for a fact." His heavy, drooping face shot a look of warning toward Artemas. "But you've come to a point of making choices and decisions, you two, and I suppose it should be decided all at once. This is more a kind of—personal matter, you might say." He directed another look toward Artemas. "Fact is, Artemas here's going to turn eighteen soon, and he's been thinking some about taking a wife. Now that this business has come up about your farm, why, what he told me was that he'd be mighty pleased and proud to have you, Jessica. That is, if you'll have him."

"No!" Behind them the back door had opened quietly and there stood Daniel, leaning against the doorframe. He was pale, and his eyes had a sunken look from the fever, but they were staring at Moses Stillwater with a piercing directness.

Artemas still sat with his arm over the back of the chair, but his expression had turned to one of shocked surprise. Daniel paid him no heed, didn't even look in his direction. He never took his eyes off Moses. Linus moved toward him as if to steady him, but Daniel's hand came up, waving him off.

" 'Clear out. Head east.' Was that what you said?"

It was a strong voice, and the words dropped like pebbles into a well.

Jessica's eyes widened and her hand flew to her cheek. *Daniel,* her lips said, but her throat was too dry. No sound came out.

Moses's face was red with barely contained rage. He turned to Artemas. "What's he doing here? I thought you told me you took care of him."

Artemas had at last come to attention, sitting forward. He began to stammer an answer, but Daniel interrupted.

" 'Clear out. Head east,' " Daniel repeated. His eyes, still on the storekeeper, had narrowed to a squint. " 'Why don't you clear out and leave the fort to the British, General van Schoyk?' " He seemed to be saying words he'd heard before, repeating them like a schoolboy reciting lessons. " 'What difference can it make to you? You're an aristocrat. You don't belong with this rabble. Clear out—head east. Go on back to the Hudson Valley and forget about this war. Let the British take over Fort Niagara. They're more your kind, anyway.' "

Moses rose slowly and stood, leaning slightly forward, his hands resting on the table as though for support. The color of a moment ago had drained from his face, and all its folds drooped. Beads of sweat stood out on his forehead. Beside him, Artemas looked pasty and scared. His eyebrows rose in two startled curves.

"I was almost sure that Sunday in spring at the service," Daniel went on. "Later, when I saw the inkwell, I knew you were the one. And hearing those words just now brought it all back as clear as the night it happened."

Linus and Jessica exchanged looks of bewilderment. Artemas darted a glance at his father.

But it was all between Daniel and Moses now, almost as if there were no one else in the cabin.

"You're General van Schoyk's son, aren't you?" Moses said with a crooked smile. "Well, he was a fool." The pleasant everyday tone had left his voice. It was hoarse and rasping now. "He was a fool, and you're another, I expect—being his son. I never had any suspicion till you stole that inkwell. But still, it was only a suspicion. I thought, no, it couldn't be. 'Twas just the work of a light-fingered boy." He shrugged, still with that twisted smile.

"That was my mother's inkwell," Daniel said. "Because of you, my mother is dead, my father is dead. You sold us out." He took a step closer. "I almost died twice because of you—once at Fort Niagara when they murdered my parents, and again the other night behind the mill. Luckily Artemas was in charge of getting rid of me the second time," he sneered. "Now you two get out of here. And keep Artemas away from Jessica."

Jessica, still sitting limply at the table, felt tears spring to her eyes, sending the whole room into a blur so that she couldn't even see the Stillwaters' departure. She had understood only a little of what had passed, and she couldn't imagine what would happen next to all of them.

But he had spoken her name.

Chapter
19

"Well—it's Peter," he said hesitantly.

"Peter." Jessica tried the name out. "Peter van Schoyk."

He nodded, and Jessica considered it. "And you're General van Schoyk's son. We've heard talk of General van Schoyk, indeed we have. But I'd sooner call you Daniel for a little while yet. Just till I get used to it."

He grinned at her, and Linus asked, "So it was really *Mr.* Stillwater who got you so riled up that Sunday at services? All this time we thought it was Artemas and what he said."

Daniel dismissed that with a wave. "No, Artemas isn't good for much, but he didn't bother me. But when I saw Stillwater I was almost certain he was the man I'd seen at Fort Niagara talking to my father."

Jessica thought back, remembering that day. "You sure got mad at all of us over it."

"I wasn't mad at you, Jessie," he said. "I just felt so helpless. I couldn't remember things clearly, I couldn't speak—"

"You could've written it out."

"I could've, but who'd have believed me? Artemas wasn't the only one who thought I was a dummy. I believe I had the whole village scared."

They stared at him as he sat on the bench, his elbows resting on the table as he talked. The sound of his voice was odd in the cabin. But it was a clear, thoughtful voice, and he spoke his words carefully, in a way that seemed to Jessica to reflect his education and background.

"Stillwater was acting as an agent, a go-between for the British, you see. The British paid him to arrange for the surrender of Fort Niagara."

Jessica remembered what her father had said weeks ago: *The British hold Fort Niagara now. And there's some strange business about that. Nobody seems to know how they came to take it so quick and easy, for it was well armed.*

"I daresay Stillwater's a man who'd make a deal with either side if the pay was good," Daniel continued. "But he didn't know my father. My father would never—" His voice wavered for a moment and then went on. "He wouldn't do it. He wouldn't sell out to Moses Stillwater and abandon the fort. Governor Tompkins appointed him a United States general and sent him out here to command, even though he wasn't a trained soldier. The governor wanted to show that there were some men of means, big landowners, who weren't siding with the British, albeit so many were. My father took that as a trust and he was bound to hold to it and defend the fort." He lowered his head and rubbed his eyes with his hand.

"But then what happened?" Linus asked.

Daniel looked up at them, his face a mask of pain. "My mother and I were with him—with my father," Daniel said in a low voice. Suddenly Jessica dreaded what he was going to say next. She remembered the day he'd turned pale and walked out of the cabin when she'd spoken about her own mother.

"We were staying in a small house some distance from the fort." His voice broke, and he swallowed and paused until he could speak again. "Father never did want us there, didn't think it was safe. He thought we should have stayed home in the Hudson Valley, but my mother wouldn't hear of it. Only after talking to Moses Stillwater, my father was really worried. He knew there'd be trouble. Just because my father refused to surrender the fort to the British didn't mean Stillwater couldn't make a deal with some other high-ranking officer at the fort."

Daniel stared straight ahead as he spoke, his eyes seeing only what had happened months ago. Linus and Jessica remained silent and waited for him to go on.

"Father convinced my mother that the two of us had to leave, and at last she agreed. So he said good-bye to us and went back to the fort, and then I left to arrange for a horse and wagon, the way he'd told me to. But when I went back for her—" He hesitated. Tears spilled from his eyes and rolled unnoticed down his cheeks. Jessica felt as if she'd stopped breathing.

"When I went back, Mother was dead, the house upside down, ransacked, the clothes she was packing strewn all over, and blood everywhere."

"Oh, Daniel." Jessica's hand came out and grabbed his.

"So I jumped in the wagon and headed for the fort to get Father, but before I even reached it, I ran into British regulars, standing where our sentries should have been. Our sentries were on the ground, and my father between them. All dead."

Nobody said anything for a minute. Then Linus said, "What'd you do?"

Daniel wiped the tears from his face and looked at them. "Jumped out of the wagon and ran at the two regulars. Just ran. I didn't know what I was doing by then. I think I was yelling. One of them whirled around toward me and swung with the butt of his rifle. Hit me on the head. I went down like a stone, I guess, and probably he reckoned he'd killed me."

"But how do you figure the British pulled it off? Took the fort?" Linus asked.

"Oh, I daresay Stillwater got to somebody else with his deal, just as my father suspected he would. That fort was quite a prize—full of arms and ammunition, food, clothing, blankets."

"But your mother—why her?" Jessica whispered.

"It wouldn't have taken more than a hint from Stillwater to let the British know about my mother and me living there. Revenge on his part, getting back at my father for refusing to make a deal with him."

"How long before you came to?" Linus was concentrating hard on the story.

"I don't know. I'm sure I was left for dead. I knew

there were bodies beside me when I woke, but I couldn't see well or even remember anything by that time, so I just got away the best I could."

Jessica realized she was still holding his hand. She started to let it go, but he held it tightly. "And pretty soon you turned up here."

They all thought back, remembering Christmas night.

"That was your mother's inkwell?" Jessica said softly.

"Yes. I took it the day I followed you into town, when Stillwater went into the back room for a minute. That was when I figured out for certain who Moses Stillwater was, and the next night I went to confront him."

"The night you left us the note," Linus said. "You shouldn't have gone alone. I'd have gone with you."

"I didn't want to involve you, but you're right, it was stupid to go alone." He looked from Linus to Jessica. "When I got to the store Moses was there by himself. I didn't tell him who I was, but I confronted him with what I knew about Fort Niagra. I should have been suspicious when he stayed so calm, but I just kept telling him how he wouldn't get away with it, how I'd tell everyone."

He shook his head at his own carelessness. "I never heard Artemas come up behind me. He grabbed me, and Moses came at me with both fists raised."

Jessica winced.

"The next thing I remember," he went on, " is waking up at Widow Cosgrove's. She told me about your pa sending word to sell the farm and that Moses was going to help you sell it, and I knew I had to get back here."

"Well, if it weren't for Jessica, you mightn't even have been here to help us," Linus said proudly. "She's the one who pulled you out of the river after Artemas dumped you down the riverbank."

Daniel turned to her. "Is that true, Jess?" They were holding hands comfortably under the table, and he gave her hand a squeeze.

Jessica blushed and tried to change the subject. She asked hesitantly, "All the time you couldn't talk—could you remember things, or was it just dark back there?"

"It was dark, but not all the time. Sometimes I remembered something quite clearly. Often at night I dreamed about it." Linus and Jessica exchanged a look, remembering the nightmare. "But when I was working, keeping busy, I let it slip right away from me. There were lots of times I'd just turn inside myself trying to get used to the fact that my parents were gone, murdered, that I'd never see them again. I'd go for long walks or sometimes just sit in the barn and think about them. Now that I can speak, I want to thank you for just letting me be during those times. I needed the time to grieve so that I could get on with what had to be done."

Linus nodded slightly and said, "You suspected Stillwater back in the spring, yet you never found your voice till today."

"Well—" Daniel glanced between them, and for the first time some of the sadness left his eyes and they took on a secret humor. "That's not exactly true. I've been talking for a while."

"Daniel!"

"You what?"

Daniel nodded. "Along about the time your father left, I got to thinking maybe if I'd try and practice, I could make myself speak again. I just didn't have any confidence, you see, that I could talk to people. But I thought I could try it alone. So that's what I did. The time I built the springhouse was the best—off by myself and no one in hearing distance."

"But we'd have helped you!" Jessica said.

"Oh, I know. But I didn't lack for listeners. Times when I'd be milking I'd talk to Bess, and I practiced on Buck and Bright and even on Floss and the kittens. At first I couldn't get the words straight or make them come out in order. But then it began to get easier. Only I still couldn't get up the courage to try it with anybody else."

"Until today," Linus said.

"Yes. Until today. And then hearing Stillwater say those same words he'd said to my father, hearing him try to persuade you to give up everything—and then even try to talk Jessie into marrying Artemas—"

Jessica felt herself turning red again. "Linus, he's tuckered out, talking so much."

"No, I'm not, Jessie. I never felt better." His glance went from one to the other. "There's something I have to show you."

With an effort, he climbed to the loft, where they heard him shuffling and moving his bedding. He came back down carefully with a small packet of envelopes in his hand.

"The day I went into the store and took the inkwell I found these. I should have given them to you that day, but I was so caught up in my own worries." He handed the packet to Jessica. "I knew it wasn't right that you never heard from your pa. Knowing what I knew about Moses Stillwater, I suspected he might be keeping these from you. I prayed he'd be in the back room long enough for me to find them, but they were right under his money box."

Jessica's heart leaped as she looked down at the familiar handwriting. "Linus, look! Letters from Pa!" She hastily wiped at the tears that blurred her vision. The three of them tore the letters open and began to read excitedly all at once.

Your mother had a small relapse. She's fine now and anxious to get back home. . . .

Dock work is mighty scarce with the war on. I'm looking at some other ways to earn some money. . . .

I've finally found work building a grand house for a merchant here in Albany. . . .

Just bring in the crops as best you can. I pray I'll be there in time for the wheat harvest, but if not, do your best. I might have a little money left over after I buy the horse and carriage to help out if we don't get it all harvested. . . .

Jessica looked at Linus and Daniel. "He never wanted us to sell the farm."

"No," Linus said. " 'Do the best you can.' " He paused. "The wheat's heading up fast. I'd call it ready."

"Good. Then let's start tomorrow," Daniel said. "I'll have my legs under me by then."

Jessica and Linus glanced at each other, and Jessica knew they were both thinking the same thing. Even though they'd heard only a tiny bit of Daniel's story, they knew enough to realize he was a rich man's son. They'd heard Alva and Solomon Justice talk of General van Schoyk—how he was one of the great Hudson Valley patroons like the Schuylers and the van Rensselaers. They owned acres without number, most leased out to tenant farmers. Likely they had barns finer than the Parishes' house.

"Harvesting wheat's a mortal hard job," Jessica said timidly. "For someone who's never done it before, it might be—" She broke off in confusion.

He looked at her and seemed amused. "Jessie, I'm the same Daniel as yesterday. Same one you bossed around pulling flax. Same one who helped with the haying and cut a whole field of corn. I can harvest wheat, too. Is it any harder than haying?"

"Oh, it's a sight harder, I'm afraid," she said worriedly. "You don't scythe it, you cradle it. And those cradles are fearful heavy. Then whoever's binding has to come behind and grab the sheaf and tie it with a binding knot."

"Can you make a binding knot?"

"I can, yes. Pa showed me how. Last year Mother and I bound behind him and Linus."

"Then we'll manage," Daniel said. "You're not going to start doubting me now, are you?"

"No, we're not," Linus said firmly. "But now you'd better rest up and get your strength back. There's a sight of work ahead of us."

Daniel agreed to rest for a while. Then he'd get up, he said, and help with chores. When he'd gone up to the loft, Jessica motioned to Linus to follow her and they slipped quietly out the back door. "Linus, does it seem right to you, what he said?"

"What?"

"You know. That he's still Daniel, same as yesterday? I mean, he isn't. He's somebody else now."

"Just because we know his right name?"

"Yes. And where he belongs." Sadness was creeping in around Jessica's heart.

Linus considered it. "Why, I don't know. He's near grown and a man, same as me. I s'pose he belongs wherever he's a mind to be."

"I don't think so, Linus. There must be property back east, maybe a great house. It's all his responsibility now."

"Well, then, if it's his, let's not us worry about it. It's his business."

"Yes, it is. You're right." But she couldn't bring herself to say the words that were really on her tongue—that she couldn't imagine the farm or the cabin or sitting down to a meal or facing any new day now without Daniel. How would she ever get used to life without him?

Chapter 20

It took no time at all for the news to get abroad. Widow Cosgrove was at the door before sunset with Leander and Asa tagging along. Jessica went outside to talk with them. They'd heard the news from Miss Ida Tate, the dressmaker, when the boys took her a basket of eggs. Mrs. Stillwater had come to pick up two dresses Miss Ida was finishing for her. In a wonderful hurry, Mrs. Stillwater was, and never even waited for Miss Ida to finish the whipstitching and hemming. She snatched the things up and left. And now the Stillwaters were gone, just up and left without a word to anyone. "They took what they could fit in their wagon—left everything in the store. Must have been mighty anxious to leave," the widow chuckled.

"Is it true?" little Asa Cosgrove interrupted shyly. "Has Daniel found his tongue?"

"He has, yes," Jessica said.

"Could we hear him?" Asa asked through the gap in his front teeth.

"We mustn't be forward," the widow cautioned.

"Go to the door," Jessica said. "He's in there."

All three of them went and pushed the door open slowly. Jessica heard Daniel call the boys by name and ask how their kitten was faring. The boys jumped with delight, and when the widow turned back to Jessica, her eyes were teary. She dabbed at them with the ragged edge of her shawl. After that she had to hear the whole story, start to finish, clucking and marveling and shaking her head at such wickedness.

"But at least you're not leavin'," she said with a sigh. "That's a mercy." She collected herself then and said that whatever day Linus fixed for starting on the wheat, they'd all come and help.

"But you have your own harvest," Linus protested.

"We'll have extra hands when we need 'em," the widow said. "Cousin Barstow from Avon said he'll come and he'll fetch along his wife's brother. We'll have hands aplenty. We'll help you with yours first. Leander's pretty near twelve and a half. He can do a good day's work."

Linus shook his head, looking remarkably like his father. "I wouldn't take work without returning it," he said.

"Well, hang it, then you can return it," the widow said. "But we'll be here to help. First thing tomorrow if you say you're ready."

Linus allowed that they were about as ready as they'd ever be.

136

After dark, by moonlight, the Reverend Mr. Baldwin came walking out to learn what had happened.

"What does it mean?" he asked anxiously. He was standing in the doorway clutching his hat. "The Stillwaters have gone. Without a by-your-leave. Loaded a wagon with all they could carry and just left. Where do you suppose—"

"Probably to Canada," Daniel said.

Pastor Baldwin stared at him. "The Lord has worked a miracle," he breathed. "Miss Ida Tate said you could speak, but I hardly dared believe it."

Linus frowned. "Why would they run away? There's a good many who stand with the British."

"You mean Stillwater—is that what he—"

They urged him to come in and take a seat, and then the story had to be told again. The minister clucked his tongue and shook his head in wonderment, both at the story and at the fact that Daniel was doing most of the telling.

Finally he said in his quiet way, "I can understand it now, why they fled. It may be so, that some hold with the British in this war, but there's a good many folks with kin in the fighting, and not so far away either. And nobody likes a man who stands on neither side—a buyer and seller of loyalties." He put his hand comfortingly over Daniel's and said, "I know nothing can make up for what Stillwater's done to your folks, or the damage he may have done by handing Fort Niagara over to the British, but I can't let this thing go." He withdrew his hand and addressed all of them. "Tomorrow I'll write to Albany and find out what can be done to apprehend him before he crosses the border. The man's a murderer and a traitor to his country, and as un-Christian as it may sound, I can't forgive him and let those crimes go unpunished."

They talked it over for a while and Jessica brought cider. Pastor Baldwin insisted, considering the letters from Alva, that he hadn't a doubt in the world that Ruth and Alva Parish would be coming home any day now. There was even some discussion about who would be the new storekeeper in the village, for surely someone would come along to fill that need, Pastor Baldwin pointed out. Then the minister questioned Daniel more closely about his loss of speech, for this seemed to fascinate him.

"I said to Alva I thought it might be his injury caused it, but there must have been more to it. Fright and grief—those kept him a prisoner of silence, too. Until you folks befriended him and made him want to live again, and speak."

A prisoner of silence. Jessica said it over in her head. How well the pastor put words together, and how right the phrase was to describe the way Daniel had been.

"And all that time," Pastor Baldwin said thoughtfully, "he was teaching himself to talk again."

Suddenly this seemed to Jessica the saddest part of all—his struggling all by himself, secretly. Practicing words on Bess as he milked, on Buck and Bright in the field, even on Floss out in the barn. All alone, not wanting anyone to hear in case he failed or his tongue hesitated. "All alone," Jessica said out loud, scarcely realizing she was doing so.

"Oh, not quite," said the minister with a smile. "None of us is ever *all* alone, isn't that so?"

Then he sighed and rose and said he must be getting back to the village, and Linus mentioned that tomorrow the Cosgroves were to help them bring in their wheat. Pastor Baldwin paused in the doorway and said in his cheerful way, "Is that a fact? You can always count on the Cosgroves, can't you? Well, count on us as well. My wife and I will be here tomorrow, too."

And before any of them could speak, he had marched out into the moonlight, headed toward the river path.

Mrs. Cosgrove, Leander, and Asa were there soon after sunup. Almost before the dew had dried, they were in the fields. The minister and his wife joined them soon after. Linus led off swinging a big toothed cradle, with Daniel and the minister following him and imitating what he did. The two of them were slow at first but picked up speed as the morning wore on. Jessica, the widow, and Mrs. Baldwin bound the wheat into shocks after them, and Leander came last, standing the shocks on end. Jessica and the widow were quick and skillful, but Mrs. Baldwin had to be shown how to twist two straws together and make a binding knot. Once shown, she worked well, and it seemed an odd thing to Jessica to see her former teacher, struggling and warm, grabbing the wheat off her husband's cradle and tying it.

Asa Cosgrove, who was only seven, kept them supplied with cool water all morning. Then at noon, with the sun beating directly on them, they sat under the apple tree and had cold meat, bread, and cider. Linus ordered Daniel to take extra rest, but Daniel insisted after a short time that his wind was holding all right and he was ready to work again.

Back in the field, the widow changed positions with Pastor Baldwin. She'd seen him favoring the blisters on his hand and she joshed him good-naturedly, as Jessica would never have dared to do, telling him if he blistered his page-turning finger he'd never be able to read his text from the Good Book at Sunday services. The widow swung the heavy cradle effortlessly, and Pastor Baldwin worked at binding.

Late in the day they stopped work and Jessica, the widow, and Mrs. Baldwin went back to the cabin to prepare food for everyone. Jessica and the widow did most of the cooking, even though Mrs. Baldwin protested she was fine.

"You'd better just set, dearie," the widow ordered. "You look pretty nigh blowed."

As they sat down to eat, Jessica said, "You've all done us such a good turn. I don't know as we can ever settle the score."

The Baldwins waved her thanks away, but the widow said briskly, "Ain't any use having neighbors unless they can help out when there's need, now is there? Someday you'll help someone else. That's the only way you ever settle the score, by passing it along."

"She's done that already," Daniel said. The heads at the table turned his way. "I mean—all the Parishes have."

They went on harvesting the next day and the next, and then it was Sabbath eve, and with most of the wheat cut and part of the oats, they all rested from their labors. On Sunday morning Jessica, Linus, and

Daniel walked into the village for services. Jessica fretted inwardly that last year's blue dress was up over her shoe tops and impossibly snug, but now she had an idea. First chance that came along, she'd take it all apart, turn it inside out and resew it, letting out the seams as she went. It was a trick she'd seen her mother do.

Pastor Baldwin, when he got to the preaching stand, clasped his hands together and gave the three of them a faint wink before he closed his eyes to pray. His face was red with sunburn.

After services there was a good bit of talk about the Stillwaters' sudden flight. Miss Ida Tate was enjoying being the center of attention in the matter. Little groups clustered around her to hear it gone over again and again. In the retelling, Miss Ida's own role in the matter was enlarged considerably, Jessica suspected.

Several men came over to Daniel and spoke to him in a friendly way. Mr. McGarrity reported that Solomon Justice and two other men had decided not to wait for a response to Pastor Baldwin's letter to Albany and were following the Stillwaters' trail out of town. The Stillwaters had headed east and then veered north toward Canada, just as Daniel had suspected. McGarrity felt confident the search party would overtake them before they reached the border.

The new settler who'd bought their white pine reported news of the war. The Americans had won a great victory under General Winfield Scott, routing the British at the Chippewa River. It was said that the Indians were deserting the British cause.

The widow pressed her hands together and said

maybe now the end of the war was in sight and Eager would be home before long.

Jessica, Linus, and Daniel walked home and spent the rest of the day quietly. Then after sundown the Sabbath was over, and Linus and Daniel went out to do some more work on the oats by moonlight while Jessica changed into an everyday dress and started taking the blue one apart by candlelight, shooing at the moths that flew in through the open door. She found that her mother had left generous seams, so it could be let out, and also the color was brighter and less faded as she turned the dress inside out. As she worked she heard for the first time the chirping of crickets. Summer was drawing to a close when you heard the crickets. Would Alva and Ruth Parish be back home before the autumn cold silenced their half-sad, half-cheerful sound?

Chapter
21

ALL THE NEXT week they were busier than ever, for suddenly the whole farm—the fields, the garden, everything around them—seemed to burst to ripeness. All of it had to be gathered in, and Jessica worried every day that something might be wasted, but the boys lent her a hand with the garden things and they worked from daylight to past dark, pulling beans and carrots, picking pumpkins and squash. While the boys picked and lugged, Jessica did the pickling, the soaking, the drying, all the saving and storing away. She had asked Widow Cosgrove's advice on the best way to preserve everything, not wanting to let anything spoil. Some things went into the cool cellar and the springhouse, some went into the loft—braids of onions now hung from the beams—but not a thing was wasted. The whole house smelled sweet with the plenty of their harvest.

Jessica wrote in her journal that night, *We never could have done this without Daniel. He seemed to be everywhere this week, always so cheerful and good-natured that he kept our spirits up. I don't like to think about the farm without him.*

Every evening, no matter how tired she was, Jessica worked for a time at turning the blue dress and restitching the seams. She had to admit, she was pleased with the results.

Then at last it was Sabbath eve again and Jessica, who'd been making cucumber pickles all day, finished the last of them and walked back to the stream to wash herself. She was tired, but she felt as if the worst was over now. There were still apples to be picked, and the dry beans had to be gathered and shelled. The potatoes weren't all dug. But she was sure they could do it now.

She brought her jar of soap with her, and while she was at it she washed her hair in the stream, letting it dry as she sat in the late afternoon sun. So much had happened since she had turned fifteen. She felt proud of the way the three of them had kept the farm going while her parents were away. It made every blister and every sore muscle worthwhile. And Daniel, talking again. In spite of all the bad that had happened to him, he was strong and healthy and had his voice back.

But thinking of Daniel made her feel sad. How much longer would he be with them? Surely he'd head back to his family estate in the Hudson Valley before long. She'd never really had a chance to sort out all the new feelings inside her, but soon it wouldn't matter one way or the other. Daniel would be gone.

The grass rustled behind her and she turned, expecting to see Boots. Daniel stood silhouetted against the evening sun.

"Jess, I—"

Jessica's heart leaped at the sound of her name on his lips. He sat down next to her and plucked a blade of grass, twirling it nervously between his fingers.

"I'll never be able to thank you—all of you—for helping me these past months," he said.

This sounded dangerously like a farewell speech to Jessica. "Oh, Daniel," she said with a lightheartedness she didn't feel. "That works both ways. Linus and I couldn't have done all this by ourselves—the crops, the springhouse, dealing with the Stillwaters. Why, just think about the—"

He interrupted her with a kiss, his hand tilting her chin up to him. Jessica closed her eyes and let her feelings wash over her. The more attached she became to Daniel, the harder it would be when he left. She pulled away slowly and a tear trickled down her cheek. Daniel brushed it away gently, seeming to understand what she was feeling. Perhaps the same thought had occurred to him, too. They sat together in silence, Daniel with his arm around her shoulder, until the sun disappeared below the horizon.

When she got back to the house, she determined not to be gloomy. She put on the blue dress she'd turned and for the first time did her hair up on top of her head instead of in its usual long braid.

When she called the boys in for supper, Daniel stood for a moment inside the doorway and said, "Well! Something's new."

Linus looked around, not finding anything different. Then he said, "Oh. The good plates. How come we're using those, Jess?"

Jessica's mouth set sternly as she looked at her brother. "I thought just for a change," she said.

Daniel said, "There's a good deal more than that changed."

Jessica felt her cheeks growing warm.

They ate and then sat and talked, satisfied at the way the week's work had gone, pleased with the good harvest, deciding what job to do next, but then coming back, as they always did, to the one thing that was never out of their minds.

"Maybe now it's near time we'll be hearing from them," Jessica said hopefully, and they all knew whom she meant.

"Well, I sent them that letter right after the Stillwaters ran off," Linus said. "The Cosgroves' relatives in Avon saw to it, so I'm sure it went east all right."

"Of course, they might be on their way already," Daniel put in. "So you really couldn't be sure the letter reached them."

"No, you couldn't be sure."

It was a conversation they'd had over and over among themselves, just as many times as they had reread the letters from Albany.

The light began to fade, and Jessica got up to clear away and wash the dishes while Linus and Daniel talked about which jobs were most important now.

"We'd better pick the apples," Linus said. "Climb up and get all the perfect ones first, then we can shake the tree. After that we'll go to work on the potatoes. No worry about them. They'll be all right clear up till frost."

"And we owe the Cosgroves some work," Daniel reminded him.

"Yes, we do. We'd better get to that right away."

"What's that?" Jessica asked sharply.

"What's what?" Linus turned his head.

"I thought I heard a wagon."

They all listened. "I hear it, too." Linus got up from his chair.

"Coming nearer," Daniel said.

Jessica felt a trembling come over her, and she had the sense to put down the two plates she was holding. The boys went to the doorway to look.

"Wagon, all right. Don't recognize the horse."

"Two people," Daniel said.

Jessica joined them and looked out. The sun was dropping lower and the figures on the wagon were two dark outlines against the sky. For a few seconds no one said anything. Then Jessica pushed past the boys and ran outside, across the dooryard, down toward the wagon track. Her heart was pounding and her feet were so light she wasn't sure they were hitting the ground.

"Ma!" she shouted. "Pa!"

"Jessica?" It was her mother's voice, excited and anxious. The wagon halted and Ruth was scrambling down, nimble as a girl, holding Jessica tightly to her. Neither one said anything. Then Ruth Parish held her daughter off at arm's length, looking at her in the soft twilight, and said, "Why, Alva, she wasn't but a girl when I left—and now look at her!"

Linus and Daniel came galloping across the dooryard. There was such a thick, muffled sound to Linus's voice that Jessica knew he was trying hard not to cry, and she was glad for the soft half darkness around them. Linus was almost seventeen, after all. They hugged and clung to each other, and then Alva said, "And this is Daniel, Ruth, the boy who's done so much to help us."

Daniel, who'd been hanging back, took a shy step forward and made a little formal bow and said, "Your servant, ma'am."

For an instant nobody said a word, only the crickets answering him, and then Ruth held out both hands to Daniel, and Alva, staring at him in disbelief, said, "What in all tarnation's going on here?"

They sat late around the table, lighting candles, talking and talking, as though everything had to be said tonight—and not just once, but two or three times over. None of them could get enough of hearing each other's voices. And over and over Alva returned to Daniel, shaking his head and marveling just as Pastor Baldwin had. "If you could've seen him, Ruth, as he was last winter. Peaked and scared and silent as a stone."

"And to think these three never got our letters until a few weeks ago—and then they went ahead anyway with the harvest—"

"The widow and her boys helped, and the Baldwins—"

"Oh, bless their hearts—"

"—but Linus said he'd never live in a city, no matter what. He'd work and save and buy his own farm—"

"Why, Linus, son, I'd never— This *is* your farm—"

"But just fancy that Moses Stillwater—what wickedness—"

On and on they talked until everyone was happily weary. The windows were exclaimed over and the stove and the new bedroom floor. "And there's something else you have to wait and see tomorrow," Jessica said, thinking of the new springhouse, which even Alva didn't know about. "Something Daniel made for us." She was pleased to see the healthy sparkle that had returned to her mother's face, the fresh color in her cheeks.

"I can't believe I'm really home." Ruth beamed at all of them.

Then at last they prepared for sleep, dragging out an extra pallet and putting it near the hearth, this time for Jessica.

Daniel objected. "I'll sleep on the hearth," he insisted. "You take your side of the loft back, Jessie."

"No need for anybody to be crowded," Linus said. "Warm night like this, Daniel and I can sleep in the barn." And so it was decided.

During the week, Daniel and Linus and Alva spent two days working at the Cosgroves' farm. Daniel seemed nervous and watchful, as if he were waiting for something to happen. Jessica assumed he was trying to figure the best time to start back east. It was so like him to wait until all his work was done and his obligations fulfilled.

Jessica spent a lot of time at the loom, keeping her eyes on the brown cloth and never stopping the rhythm of the shuttle. She felt rather than saw that her mother took her eyes from her knitting, quick fingers pausing as she looked at her daughter's face.

"You've gotten pretty fond of Daniel, haven't you, Jess?" her mother said. "It's no wonder. He's a nice boy, and you three have been through a lot together."

"Oh, Ma," Jessica blurted tearily. "I never felt this way about anyone before. I don't know what I'll do when he leaves."

"I understand," Ruth said, getting up to come put her arms around her daughter. "The time I spent in Albany away from your pa and you and Linus was the hardest time of my life. But here we are, all together again, just as it was meant to be." She stroked Jessica's hair. "Things have a way of working out, Jess. I don't believe for one minute that Daniel will disappear from our lives forever."

Jessica looked hopefully at her mother. More than anything, she wanted to believe that what Ruth said was true.

Jessica didn't see Daniel alone again until late afternoon the next day, when she carried the milk out to the springhouse. Then, as she fastened the door behind her to return to the cabin, she saw him walking along the path toward her.

"I thought this was where I'd find you," he said.

"I'll think of you whenever I come out here," she said, trying to keep her voice light and not give away the sadness she was really feeling. "This springhouse is a real wonder. I can't remember how we ever managed without it."

They walked along together. "Jess, I need to talk to you," Daniel said.

Jessica's heart filled with dread, but she said evenly, "All right, Daniel. Let's sit here next to the stream."

Daniel seemed nervous, as if he didn't know how to begin. "You remember the letter you and Linus sent to Albany with the Cosgroves' relatives?" He was looking at the ground. "Well, I sent a letter with them, too. Not to Albany—to my grandfather in Rhinebeck."

Jessica knew what was coming and fought the urge to get up and run.

"I wanted to let him know I was alive," Daniel went on. "And to tell him I wouldn't be coming back."

Jessica turned to him, wondering if she had heard him right. He glanced up at her, then quickly back at the ground, as if the words he needed to say were written there in the dirt.

"I told him I wanted to make a life for myself in western New York, to build something of my own, the way he did so many years ago." He pulled an envelope from his pocket and removed and unfolded the paper inside. "I got a letter from Grandfather today. There's a lot in here about my mother and father, and how my being alive is the answer to his prayers." He smiled self-consciously. "Says he plans to personally see that Moses Stillwater gets everything that's coming to him." He paused, scanning the letter. "Then he says that he admires my spunk. He says he's often thought that the property should be broken up and sold off in smaller parcels. He thinks that's the way the country is going, and so do I. Small, independent holdings. He wants me to have part of the money from selling the land—help me get started."

Daniel is staying here? He isn't leaving? Jessica wondered how long it would take for her to accept and believe what he had just told her. For weeks she'd been getting ready for him to leave, for adjusting to life without him. It was too much to take in all at once.

"The thing is, Jess," he said, taking her hand, "I don't want to do any of this—without you." He swallowed and said, "Jessica, will you marry me?"

Jessica was speechless. "I—I . . . y-you mean . . . ," she stammered.

He must have taken this as a rejection, for dismay and disappointment clouded his features. "Oh, not right now," he said hastily. "In a year or so, when I've got my property and can make a proper home. I'll be eighteen by then." He searched her face hopefully. "I've already talked to your pa," he admitted. "He said it was your decision."

Jessica took a deep breath, and her jumbled emotions quietly fell into place. "Yes . . . Peter. I'll marry you."

He smiled broadly and threw his arms around her. "Come on," he said, "let's go make a proper announcement."

Hand in hand they headed down the path through the golden afternoon sunshine toward the cabin.